Georgie's Moon

✷

Also by Chris Woodworth

*

When Ratboy Lived Next Door

Georgie's Moon

CHRIS WOODWORTH

Farrar, Straus and Giroux
New York

The author gratefully acknowledges Dr. Steven L. Burg,
Adlai E. Stevenson Professor of International Politics, Brandeis University,
for his critical reading of the manuscript.

Distributed in Canada by Douglas & McIntyre Ltd.
Printed in the United States of America
Designed by Abby Kagan
First edition, 2006
1   3   5   7   9   10   8   6   4   2

www.fsgkidsbooks.com

Library of Congress Cataloging-in-Publication Data
Woodworth, Chris, date.
    Georgie's Moon / Chris Woodworth.— 1st ed.
        p.   cm.
    Summary: With a chip on her shoulder and a talent for disruption,
seventh-grader Georgie Collins moves with her mom to a small Indiana
town, where they await the return of Georgie's father from Vietnam.
    ISBN-13: 978-0-374-33306-5
    ISBN-10: 0-374-33306-8
    [1. Fathers and daughters—Fiction.   2. Vietnamese Conflict,
1961–1975—Fiction.   3. Friendship—Fiction.   4. Middle schools—
Fiction.   5. Schools—Fiction.]   I. Title.

PZ7.W8794 Geo 2006
[Fic]—dc22

                                                                2005040147

To Beverly Reingold,

for seeing the story I should write,

and to

Mark Woodworth,

for encouraging me to write it

Georgie's Moon

✴

"Georgia?"

Instead of answering the school secretary, Georgie stared at the shiny plaque mounted on the freshly painted wall:

GLENDALE MIDDLE SCHOOL, ESTABLISHED 1970

Georgie had been to a lot of schools, but this was the first new one.

When she didn't respond, the school secretary called out, "Georgia Collins?"

Two other girls were also in the office waiting area. Georgie leaned forward and looked at them as if to see if one could be a girl named Georgia Collins. Then she looked at the secretary and shrugged.

The secretary puckered her forehead and disappeared into the guidance counselor's office.

It was a momentary reprieve, but it made Georgie feel a little better.

School started in one week and Georgie had come to pay her book rental fees. After taking her money, the man at the school bookstore had ripped off a note stapled to her form and handed it to her. "Says you're to go to the guidance office and see the counselor, Mrs. Donovan."

"Why?" Georgie asked.

He shrugged. "Guess you'll find out when you get there."

Only kids marked as troublemakers were sent to the guidance office, and school hadn't even started yet!

Georgie had made her way through the maze of unfamiliar halls to the office, but she didn't want to be there. No way was she going to make this easy on the secretary.

The secretary came back, followed by a tall woman in a jacket and skirt.

"Georgie, I'm Mrs. Donovan. Would you please come in now?"

"Sure thing," Georgie said, giving the secretary a wide smile as she walked by. The secretary stared at her with her jaw hanging. Georgie had the urge to put her hand beneath the woman's chin and close her mouth. She didn't do it, but urges were always hard to resist.

Mrs. Donovan's desk faced the wall, so that when she

turned her chair around, it became part of a circle of empty chairs. She said, "Please sit down, Georgie. Anywhere is fine."

Georgie had already pulled out a chair, but when Mrs. Donovan said to sit, she threw her new books onto the chair instead.

Georgie could see her little game. "Anywhere is fine," as if it would be just dandy if she chose Mrs. Donovan's chair. It was a "We're friends" game. Well, Georgie was onto it and she wasn't falling into any traps.

She walked over to a set of shelves displaying trophies and books. In the very center, with a little spotlight on it, lay a bottle with a ship inside.

Mrs. Donovan said, "Feel free to pick up anything you see."

Georgie turned away from the shelves and sat down.

Mrs. Donovan let out a little breath and sat down, too. "How do you like it here at Glendale?" she asked.

"How did you put the ship inside the bottle?" was Georgie's answer.

"My father did it, actually. He made each tiny piece that you see. Then he placed them through the neck of the bottle. It took forever to build because his hands couldn't fit inside. He used special, long tools that were awkward to work with."

Mrs. Donovan walked over and picked up the bottle. She gently rubbed her hand over it. "I used to watch him for hours. It was such hard work. Yet when people asked him how he built it, he always just said, 'A little at a time.' I was amazed that he made it sound so simple."

When Georgie didn't say anything, Mrs. Donovan put the bottle back on the shelf.

"He passed away two years ago," she said. "I still miss him terribly." She sat down again. "So, I told you about my dad. Why don't you tell me about yours?"

Georgie picked up Mrs. Donovan's letter opener from her desk and turned it over in her hand. "He's a major in the Air Force, stationed in Vietnam."

"And?" Mrs. Donovan prompted.

"And he doesn't build boats in bottles."

Mrs. Donovan sat back, waiting. Finally she said, "Georgie, your mother was here last week. We had a long talk about you. We also talked about your father."

Georgie stared at the bridge of Mrs. Donovan's nose. She wore glasses, so it was easier to find a spot on the nosepiece to look at. Georgie let her eyes sort of relax. When Mrs. Donovan became blurry, Georgie felt detached. She tried this at home, but it was harder with Mom. For one thing, Mom had a way of looking around the room when she talked. And she didn't wear glasses. The nosepiece was a definite plus.

Mrs. Donovan's voice finally reached her.

"Georgie? Did you hear anything I said?"

"Yes, of course, Mrs. Donovan. May I go now?"

"Yes, Georgie." She sighed. "But I do hope that once

school gets under way, you'll drop in any time you feel like talking."

She followed Georgie into the waiting area. The secretary gave Georgie a look that would have wilted a weaker person. Georgie winked at her.

The secretary blinked, caught off guard again. She turned her back to Georgie and said, "Mrs. Donovan, here is the file you requested."

"Thank you, Mrs. Sanders."

"Oops!" Georgie said, and quickly turned around. "Forgot my books in your office. Can I get them?"

Mrs. Donovan said, "Certainly," as she scanned the report.

She was so trusting, not coming back in with Georgie, just as Georgie had suspected she would be. It took Georgie only a minute to do what she needed to do. Then she picked up her books and went out to the waiting area.

"Mrs. Donovan? Thanks. I feel a lot better now."

"Well! That's wonderful, Georgie," she said in a surprised voice.

Georgie walked around the corner and peeked back. When Mrs. Donovan reached her office, she stopped dead in the doorway and let out a small cry. Georgie hefted her books and headed down the hall. She knew that Mrs. Donovan had seen her dad's bottle on her desk, where Georgie had put it. The cork had been removed and her letter opener had been rammed into the center of the bottle, cutting off the ship's mast.

2 "Ouch!" Georgie cried out as she pulled the baby's sticky fingers from her hair.

She looked into the baby's blue eyes. "Shannon? Or are you Jennifer? Whoever you are, you're the reason I'm never having kids."

The baby squealed and reached for Georgie's hair again. Georgie quickly sat her down on the picnic blanket, hard enough that she heard the diaper squish.

Georgie wiped her sweaty forehead with her arm, peeking under it to see if Mom had noticed. Mom was struggling to lift the playpen out of the station wagon, so she couldn't have heard. Georgie decided to pretend she hadn't, either. Changing diapers was definitely not Georgie's bag.

"She's wet."

Georgie looked at John, who was three and a tattletale.

"No, she's not. I made that sound, see?" Georgie tried to make squishing sounds with her mouth.

"Uh-uh." He shook his head.

"John?" Georgie wiggled her finger, beckoning him to come closer. He squeezed a toy truck to his chest and continued shaking his head.

"But it's important," Georgie said.

John took a step back, away from her.

"Okay, fine. I'll tell someone else."

John blinked his eyes. When Georgie acted as if she was going to leave, he slowly walked toward her.

Georgie waited until he was right in front of her. She leaned toward him and shouted, "Scram!"

The toy truck flew up and John fell flat on his behind. The truck bounced between his sprawled legs.

Georgie howled with laughter. Today might not be so bad after all.

Georgie's mom straightened from the playpen and said, "Whew! That was work, but it will keep the little ones from roaming. What was that yelling I heard?"

"John and I were playing."

John grabbed his truck and ran behind the playpen. Georgie had to give him credit for not crying. Maybe he wasn't a totally worthless snot.

Georgie's mom gathered up the three youngest kids and settled them inside the playpen.

"Tell me again why we had to bring these brats here," Georgie said. "And why we had to come at all."

Mom sat beside her. They had the same thick, brown hair that stuck out in every direction, but that was all Georgie had inherited from her. Georgie had grown taller than Mom a year ago and Mom was—well, she wasn't *fat*, just sort of round. Dad always said she was soft, in exactly the right way.

"Sugar," she said, "if we're going to live here, I think it's important to take part in the town's celebration."

"You sound like we're gonna stay here. No one has officially decided that, Mom."

"No, but maybe we *should* officially decide that." She reached one arm around Georgie to give her a squeeze. Georgie leaned forward to get a banana out of the picnic basket. She didn't want the banana, but she wanted the squeeze even less.

"It's a nice place," Mom said. "And they don't have a preschool. You know the plan has always been—"

Georgie cut in. "That when Dad comes home from Vietnam and is discharged from the Air Force, we will *all* decide where to live. Then you can start a preschool. I know the plan, Mom."

"Yes, that was the plan." Georgie's mom lifted her heavy hair from her neck. She softly said, "And your dad liked this place when we moved here, so—"

"Okay, okay, I get your point."

One of the babies began crying, and Mom reached into the playpen to pick her up.

"So we're here for the town's party," Georgie said. "But why did we have to bring the brat brigade?"

"Shhh," Mom said. "Don't call them that. And you already know why. Until I get the preschool up and running, I babysit."

"But Labor Day is a holiday. A *holiday*," Georgie repeated for emphasis. "You have them all week. This is your day off."

"And their parents are paying me double because it's a holiday."

Georgie shook her head, then looked around at all the families on blankets with their grills set up and radios blaring. According to the newspaper, years ago there were two small towns side by side, Glendale and North Ridge. Over time they kept growing until you couldn't tell one from the other. Now North Ridge was officially merged into Glendale. They had become one town, and this was the big celebration, a huge picnic and a ceremony with the mayor and all the town bigwigs, followed by fireworks later.

Georgie couldn't care less. The only thing that affected her was the new middle school, which combined the two old ones. She would be a seventh-grader there, starting tomorrow.

Georgie's family had moved to Glendale, Indiana, at the end of May, and it had seemed like the perfect place. With Dad's family from Georgia and Mom's from Wisconsin, it felt right to be in the middle. Dad liked that Glendale wasn't too far from Grissom Air Force Base, and Mom liked that it was far enough away that she wasn't *on* base. Plus, with the schools consolidating, all the students would have to get to know those from the other school. Georgie wouldn't be the only "new" kid this time.

It didn't matter that this town had seemed perfect when they moved here. Right now she hated it. She hated these cookie-crumb-crunchers that her mother babysat. She hated everyone she saw, stopping just short of her mother. She couldn't do that. But lately even Mom had been hard to take.

She reminded herself that it wasn't easy for Mom to be married to a soldier. Mom was so gentle. She actually loved the little snotbags, even though they belonged to someone else. Mom couldn't have more kids, but Georgie knew Mom wanted them by the sad look in her eyes whenever someone asked why she had only one. If it happened when Dad was there, he would wrap an arm around Mom and say, "It's not like we could have improved on perfection. We got it right the first time, right, darlin'?"

Georgie felt warm whenever he said that. But Mom probably would have had a dozen of her own if she could have.

Georgie stretched. She needed to get away from Mom and the kids for a little while. Then she wouldn't be so moody. No one had to tell her that on the outside everything was fine today. It was Georgie's insides that were all mixed up.

"I'm going to walk around," she said to her mother.

"First hand me a diaper, please. The baby is soaked through."

Georgie opened the back of the station wagon. Heat wafted from the inside of the car as she picked up a cloth diaper from the neat stack. She also got out the bucket and lid that would hold the dirty diapers.

Another reason not to have kids, she told herself. Not

unless they made a diaper you could throw away instead of swirling it around in the toilet to get the crap out. Georgie couldn't even take a pee at home without removing a soaking diaper from the toilet first.

"Thanks, sugar," her mom said. "And take John with you, okay?"

"Aw!" Georgie said, but Mom handed Georgie the strap. John could run off quicker than a jackrabbit if you didn't keep a close eye on him.

Georgie jerked the strap from her mom, slipping one end around John's wrist and the other around hers. So much for getting into a better mood.

She walked, half dragging John. The smell of barbecue smoke was heavy in the air. The entire park was full of cars pulled over to the side with blankets on the ground. Food was spread out on tailgates and small grills were set up.

She came upon what looked like a typical family. There was a mother and a teenage girl setting out a picnic dinner. There was another girl about Georgie's age, a boy a little younger messing with a toy airplane, and a dad barbecuing. Georgie felt that familiar tightening in her throat as she watched the dad. His hair was cut short like her own father's. She swallowed to lessen the feeling she always got when she missed her dad. Instead, she focused on the skinny girl with long blond hair who was crouched low and seemed to be backing away from the family a little at a time.

Georgie sat Indian-style on the grass and tried her best to concentrate on the girl and ignore John's whining. She waited until the girl slipped beneath the long branches of a willow tree. When she didn't come back out, Georgie said, "C'mon," and pulled John over to the tree where she last saw the girl.

"Wait here," Georgie told John.

"No!" John stuck out his bottom lip.

"Play with your truck. I'm not leaving, see?" She held up her end of the strap. When John seemed satisfied that she wouldn't be far, Georgie poked her head through the veil of branches.

"Hey!" she said. The girl jumped. It always gave Georgie a little thrill to catch people off guard.

"What are you doing here?" Georgie said. "Did you steal something?"

"Oh, no," the girl said. "It's nothing like that."

"Well, what is it, then?"

"I was, um, just resting."

Georgie stared into the girl's eyes, waiting. Her face flushed and she looked away. "I was just watching my family over there," she finally said.

Georgie usually knew when somebody was telling the truth. She decided the girl was, so she stopped staring at her face. She gave the rest of her a once-over, though, looking for a peace sign or a "flower power" button. Anything to tell her if this girl was another one of those hippie radicals against the Vietnam War. When she didn't see any, she relaxed.

"So, what's your name?"

"Lisa. Lisa Loutzenhiser."

Georgie laughed. "What kind of name is *that*?"

Lisa winced. "I don't know. My parents aren't into genealogy."

"Too bad. You probably get that a lot."

"Yeah. From everyone."

"I'm Georgia Collins, but I like to be called Georgie."

Georgie sat down next to Lisa. "Looks like you could watch your family any old time, but it's cool with me if that's what you want to do." Georgie looked over at them. "They're easy to pick out, that's for sure. Every one of you is skinny and blond. That must be your dad by the barbecue."

"Right," Lisa said.

"Is he a soldier?"

Lisa looked at her. "What makes you ask that?"

"The hair. It's a military buzz. Plus he carries himself so straight."

"He's not now, but he used to be in the Army. He never changed his hair, I suppose. You're a pretty good guesser."

"Not really. My dad's in the Air Force."

"Oh." Lisa looked away. "Is he stationed here?"

"No," Georgie said. "Vietnam."

Lisa tucked her hair behind her ears. "That must be hard."

"Yeah, we moved here last May, then he shipped out." Georgie looked back at Lisa's family. "And your mom is setting out food on the blanket, right? Is that girl your sister?"

"Uh-huh, Carla. She's going to college next week."

"And the boy?"

"That's Denny," Lisa said. Georgie liked the way Lisa's eyes came to life when she said his name.

"Denny, huh? Is he your favorite?"

"Gosh, no! Carla's my favorite! And Alan. He's my older brother. Denny's the world's biggest brat."

Georgie laughed. "Okay, so there's Carla, Denny, and Alan. Where's Alan?"

Lisa pulled at a long strand of hair. "He's . . . not here."

From the other side of the willow branches Georgie heard, "Georgie, wanna go *now*!"

Then Georgie got yanked backward.

Lisa looked at the leash pulling Georgie's arm and said, "Are you walking your dog?"

Georgie raised her eyebrows. "You think dogs can talk?" She parted the willow branches to show John to Lisa.

"John, knock it off or I'll tie you to one of the fireworks," Georgie said. "You'll explode all over town."

John's face scrunched up to cry. "Georgie, you can't!"

"I won't, as long as you're good," Georgie said. She turned back to Lisa. "So, where do you go to school?"

"I live on the North Ridge side, but I'm in middle school and this year they're consolidating with—"

"Glendale! That's where we live. Are you in seventh grade?"

Lisa nodded.

"Me, too! Far out."

John began crying in earnest now.

Georgie said, "I've got to get this crybaby back to Mom. Maybe I'll see you at school, Lisa Loutzenhiser, whose family doesn't care who they are."

Lisa called out, "I didn't say that."

But Georgie didn't answer. She had already backed out of the branches and was heading toward Mom with John in tow.

Later, after everyone had been fed and the parents had finally come to collect their kids, Georgie and Mom were able to relax. Georgie lay back on one elbow and gazed at the moon, thinking of her father. When Dad left for Vietnam, he had taken her outside and said in his soft Southern drawl, "You see that moon up there? When it's night in Vietnam, it's daytime here."

"I know," Georgie had said.

"Do you realize that means I'll see the moon before you do?" He'd taken her hands and said, "So if you start missin' me, just look up because every night I'll send my love to you on the moon."

And every night she had looked up. A full moon was Georgie's favorite, filling her with hope and love for her dad. But tonight's was a first-quarter moon, only halfway to plumping its way back to full.

One by one, the bright explosions of fireworks took over the sky. Georgie rolled onto her stomach and stared at the stand of willow trees.

"A penny for your thoughts, sugar," Mom said. She always said dumb stuff like that, trying to get into Georgie's mind.

"I don't have a thought in my head, Mom," Georgie said. But that wasn't true. She was thinking that the only thing weirder about that girl Lisa hiding from her family all that time was how they just went about their business, as if they never once noticed she was gone.

3 Georgie checked the room number against her schedule. They both read "J-3." She put her hand on her stomach, trying to quiet the heaving sensation before going inside. It was the same feeling she got on a roller coaster. Riding roller coasters and going to new schools—they never got any easier, but Georgie had learned not to let it show. She took a deep breath and sauntered into her homeroom as if she'd been going there for years. She chose a seat where she could get a good look at the door, because a good surveillance post is always an advantage.

Slowly the room began filling with kids, dazed from fighting new lockers and searching for classrooms. Georgie knew that's how she usually looked, but this time *everyone* was a new student. It was almost fun to sit back and watch the kids coming in, with their eyes darting around and arms close to their bodies, as if they were afraid they had B.O.

One of the last to walk in was the girl from the park yesterday. What was her name? Lisa. Lisa something-weird.

Lisa walked to a desk and swung her long blond hair behind her without taking her hands off her books. Girls like that always fascinated Georgie. The kind who could grab a rubberband off a rolled newspaper and use it to whip her hair into a perfect ponytail without ever looking in a mirror. Georgie had to keep her own wayward, wiry strands under a bandana or hat of some sort.

A boy walked by and said, "Hi, Loutzenhiser."

Loutzenhiser! That was it. Georgie repeated it to herself so she would remember.

Lisa pulled her hair behind her ears and softly said, "Hi, Craig."

Yuck. Why didn't she just announce her crush on him over the PA system? The way her head ducked and her face turned pink said it anyway.

Georgie looked the boy over. Craig had hair that curled up at his collar and bangs in his eyes, just like that singer everybody thought was so cute, Bobby Sherman. Craig was too well kept, too . . . soft . . . to be Georgie's type. But then, Georgie wasn't sure she had a type. One thing she knew for sure, though, was that if she ever liked a boy, she wasn't going to like one who was prettier than she was. Plus he wore a leather string around his neck with a peace sign hanging from it. Definitely not her type.

The bell rang and everyone scrambled to a seat.

"Hello, class. I'm Miss Horton and I'll be your homeroom teacher. I've taught math at Glendale Middle School for twenty-three years."

The teacher hesitated and craned her long neck around the room. She smiled as if she were waiting for applause.

"Of course, this year is a little different, isn't it? This is our first year with North Ridge. I'm sure you all know that merging the two schools wasn't a popular idea among many of the citizens of Glendale—particularly citizens who live on the North Ridge side of town."

"Try riding a bus all that way and see how you feel!" someone yelled from the back of the classroom.

The entire class began talking at once. Georgie was already sick of people complaining about the two towns merging and she had lived here only a few months.

Miss Horton clapped her hands until the room was quiet again. "We realize it will be a little difficult at first. The staff here at Glendale Middle School understands that you used to be rival schools and now you're one and the same. At least we have this lovely new building! And Principal Gordon has come up with a fun idea for us to get to know one another."

When was a principal's idea ever fun? Georgie opened her notebook with a big flip and began drawing a picture of a giraffe's body with Miss Horton's head. The guy beside Georgie saw it and smiled at her. He motioned to the kids behind him to look at it.

"This homeroom has an equal number of students from

Glendale and North Ridge and—" Miss Horton stopped when she heard the kids snickering at Georgie's drawing. "Excuse me, when a teacher is talking we listen."

Georgie kept her head down. With a touch a magician would admire, she slid the page to a clean sheet and scribbled.

"Young lady, did you hear me?" Miss Horton asked. "What's your name?"

Georgie looked up and said, "Yes, I heard you. My name is Georgia Collins."

"Then repeat what I said, Georgia Collins."

"You said"—Georgie sat tall and raised her voice high, like Miss Horton's—"when a teacher is talking we listen."

Miss Horton's eyes bulged out of her bony face. Georgie loved it when teachers went berserk, and Miss Horton looked about to blow. Still, it *was* her first day. No sense in making unnecessary enemies.

"But we *are* allowed to take notes, right?" Georgie gave Mrs. Horton a huge smile that was as fake as pink fur. "I wanted to make sure I got down all the details of this fun way of getting to know one another."

Georgie held up her notebook to show the words *Fun* and *Getting acquainted.*

"Oh!" Miss Horton chirped. "Well, yes, that's fine." Her hand stroked her throat and she wore a confused look, as if she knew she'd been tricked but wasn't sure how.

"As I was saying, there is a chart in front of the principal's office. Each student from North Ridge will be paired with a student from Glendale. It's a way to not only get acquainted but also help our newly formed town. We're calling the program Good Deeds for Glendale. I'm sure you'll find there are a lot of pleasant projects."

She picked up a stack of papers. "Principal Gordon is giving everyone until the end of the week to find someone from the other school to work with. If you haven't signed up by then, you will be paired with another student."

Groans rose from the back of the room.

"I know this is something new and new things often don't sound appealing. But it will be a very easy way for you to improve your English and health grades."

Miss Horton began passing out mimeographed sheets. Georgie picked up her paper and breathed in the sharp, sweet smell of the blue ink.

"As you can see, you will be expected to turn in a joint report on the good deed you performed as a team in six weeks—the end of the first grading period."

Georgie was listening closely to Miss Horton.

"This report will count toward half of your English grade. A log of the time you spent working on your assignment and its outcome—as well as how your relationship with your partner evolves—will be considered a health experiment and will count toward half of your health grade."

"Wait a minute," the boy next to Lisa said. "You mean that if we don't do this, we'll get an F for half of our English *and* health grades?"

"That's exactly right." Miss Horton raised her head

and squeezed the rest of the mimeographs against her scrawny chest.

A chorus of "That stinks!" and "You've got to be kidding me!" rang out.

Miss Horton clapped her hands. "Remember, people, attitude is everything! Think *fun* and it will be!"

Beneath *Fun* Georgie wrote in her notebook, "Think stupid and it will be!"

Lisa gathered her books to leave and Georgie fell into step with her.

"Hey, you're Lisa Loutzenhiser, right?"

"Right!" She was obviously pleased that Georgie had remembered her name. "How's your little brother?" she asked.

"I don't have a brother," Georgie said.

"But—" Lisa stammered. "At the park. What was his name? John!"

"Oh, my mother babysits. I was helping her out. You'd be surprised how many people want to dump their kids on someone else."

A girl walking from the other direction pushed her shoulder into Lisa, nearly knocking her down.

"Oh, sorry," Lisa said, even though it hadn't been her fault.

The girl asked in a voice that was practically arctic, "So, Lisa, how does *Alan* like his new home?"

"Um, I don't know," Lisa answered as she hurried away.

"Who was that?" Georgie asked, keeping up with her.

"That was Kathy Newman. We used to be best friends."

"Used to be?"

"Well, yeah, you know. Things change." Lisa stopped at her locker.

"She ran into you and *you* apologized," Georgie said.

"I know," Lisa said. "I—I don't want to talk about it." She tried to work the combination, but her fingers looked clumsy.

"Need help?" Georgie asked.

"No. It's just that these new locks are kind of stiff, don't you think?"

"I didn't have a problem with mine," Georgie said. Deep down, she suspected that Lisa was concentrating on her locker combination to give herself time to recover from seeing this Kathy person. It was a good stalling maneuver and Georgie admired her for it, so she decided to let the subject drop.

"Ready?" Georgie said when Lisa had gathered her books.

"Yes," Lisa said. "So you're from Glendale and I'm from North Ridge."

"Yeah. So?"

"So we could be partners. I mean, if you want to."

"I could be partners with anyone in this building. I just moved here, remember? I don't know anyone. The last school I went to was in Illinois," Georgie said. She stopped at the principal's office. "Hey, want to have a laugh?"

"Sure," Lisa said.

Georgie walked over to the sign-up poster listing the options for Good Deeds for Glendale. She ran her finger down the selections: "Former First Lady Lady Bird Johnson's call to Keep America Beautiful. Probably picking up trash. Then there's Animal Care, Health Care, Tutoring—don't you love how vague they are?"

"Animal Care might be pet sitting. That could be fun."

"It might be mucking horse crap out of a stall, too," Georgie said, making a face.

"We have to sign up. I mean, she said they would pair us with someone if we didn't."

"Right. So we sign up." Georgie grabbed the pencil that was swinging from a string and wrote under Health Care, "Georgia Collins and Ringo Starr."

"Ringo Starr!" Lisa laughed.

"Too well known?" Georgie asked. She erased the name and said, "Wait, I read that his real name is Richard Starkey." She penciled it in.

Then she asked, "How do you spell your last name?"

"Umm, L-o-u-t-z-e-n-h-i-s-e-r."

A boy stood next to Georgie, looking at the poster. He said, "What kind of name is that?"

Georgie answered, "Spanish. Geez, I can't believe you didn't know that."

The boy shrugged and left.

Lisa laughed. "Thanks! I hate the attention my last name gets."

"No problem," Georgie said. "Just remember, when someone says something you don't like, snap right back. It throws them off guard."

What was it about this girl that made Georgie want to toughen her up?

"What's your favorite song?" Georgie asked.

"I guess it's 'Bridge over Troubled Water,' " Lisa said.

"Oh! Good one. Simon and Garfunkel." Georgie thought a moment. "Instead of Paul Simon or Art Garfunkel, we'll combine their names." Then she wrote: "Lisa Loutzenhiser and Simon Garfunkel."

"Oh, Georgie! I can't do that!" Lisa said.

"They probably won't even catch on," Georgie said.

"But I don't understand," Lisa said. "We'll still have to do the project, right?"

"I suppose." Georgie sighed. "But we won't have to work with a real partner. There'll be no one to rat on us if we don't want to work on it every week. And best of all, it'll be fun to see if they figure it out."

Lisa squeezed her books tight and tried to act cool about the whole thing. Georgie could tell it was a struggle.

"I don't think I'll do that. No offense." Lisa erased "Simon Garfunkel."

Well, Georgie definitely didn't want to be stuck with some dud friend. She decided to throw out a little test to see if Lisa was the type of person she wanted to be around.

"Let me guess," Georgie said. "You're one of those rule followers, aren't you? Teacher's pet. That kind of person?"

Lisa twisted the string around the pencil. "No, I'm not a rule follower *all* the time."

"So, what about this time?"

Lisa hesitated a couple of seconds, then wrote Richard Starkey over the erased spot next to her name. "Loutzenhiser and Garfunkel are both unusual names. We'll have to switch imaginary partners to not draw attention."

Georgie smiled. This time for real.

The worst part of Georgie's day should have been the best—going home. It was 3:45 and the babies would be waking from their naps. It would be another two hours before the last monster went home.

She took a deep breath at the back door and walked into the kitchen.

"Hi, sugar!" Mom called. "How was your day?"

Georgie followed her mother's voice into the living room. A couch was positioned at one end, the television at the other, and on each side Mom had squeezed in two cribs. Georgie looked in at Mom, sitting in the middle of the floor with babies swarming over her like ants on a dropped cookie. "Probably not as exciting and fun-filled as a day of babysitting," she said dryly.

"Oh, we had a fine day! Jennifer said her first word! Of course, I can't tell her mommy. She'd be so upset that she missed it. I'll wait until Jennifer says it at home." Mom picked up the baby and blew raspberries on her tummy, then said in baby talk, "She'll have such a surprise, won't she, Jenny-girl?"

"Yuck," Georgie said. She walked back into the kitchen and reached above the cabinet, where she kept her snacks hidden from the little kids.

John jumped out from under the kitchen table. He was wearing a metal strainer on his head as a helmet. "Pop! Pop! Pop!" He fired his cap gun at Georgie, who ignored him. "You're dead!" he yelled.

"You're wrong," she said without looking at him.

"I'm not!" he said. "I shot you! Now fall down!"

"One, I knew you were there. Two, your aim was off. If that had been a real gun, you would have missed me. And most important of all is three, which is that you just have a junky toy gun, so I'm not dead and I'm not falling down," she said. His lower lip stuck out. What a sissy.

"I'll be in my room," she called, and slammed the door, drowning out whatever Mom was saying. Why couldn't her mother be like other women? If she wanted to work, fine, but do it someplace else. It was getting so Georgie couldn't even eat an apple without checking for teeth marks and spit.

She threw her books on the bed and stretched out. Her room was the only place in the house where she found any peace, because it was the only room that was off-limits to the brat brigade. Georgie loved her room. It was painted a nice, solid blue. She'd had to fight Mom on that one.

"Oh, Georgie, blue is a boy's color," she'd said.

But Dad had been home when they'd moved in and he'd said, "Blue's a fine color. And how can it be just a boy's color when it's the color of my girl's eyes?"

Georgie had smiled at him, her blue eyes looking into his identical ones.

"You two!" Mom had said. "Do I get my way with anything around here?"

Dad had wrapped his arms around Mom. "Darlin', you can always have your way with me." He'd nuzzled her neck. Mom had giggled. Georgie had acted embarrassed, but she wasn't really.

"And I want to paint a map of Vietnam here." Georgie had spread her arms across one wall.

"Now, why would you want to do that, Captain?" Dad had said.

"So I can mark where you've been from your letters."

His eyes had crinkled in the corners and he'd shaken his head. "I don't know, hon. Seems like a lot of work. Besides, who'd want to stare at a place where all that fightin's going on when they're fallin' asleep?"

"I would," Georgie had said. "Because that's where you'll be."

"Well, it's your room. It's up to you," he'd said.

Later, after she'd outlined the country on the wall, he'd

bought a can of pale yellow paint. He had helped her paint it, then written in the names of the cities and places that he knew.

Georgie looked at the map now. If she squinted, North Vietnam looked a little like a kite and South Vietnam, a wide ribbon blowing, trying to break free. She had glued little red stars to the places Dad had sent letters from. And every night she watched the news. They always showed the war. Each night she searched the faces of soldiers on the television screen, always hoping for a glimpse of her dad. She marked the places mentioned on TV in silver stars because she knew American soldiers had been there, even if she didn't know whether Dad was one of them. She had more silver stars than red, many more, but she tried not to think about that.

She was just finishing her homework when Mom knocked on the door.

"Sweet pea? Coast is clear. You can come out now."

Georgie stretched, then stuck her head out the door. "Are the curtain-climbers gone? Even John?" Sometimes John's mom worked late.

"Even John." Mom laughed.

Georgie followed Mom into the living room.

"Now we can talk." Mom patted the couch. "Come sit beside me."

"I'm kind of hungry." Georgie walked toward the kitchen. "How about we eat?"

Mom sighed. "Georgie, it's your first day in a new school. Bear with your mean old mom who just wants to know how it went."

"It went fine. Just dandy." Georgie opened the refrigerator door.

Mom came into the kitchen. "Okay, how about you help me cook? We'll talk at the same time."

Georgie rolled her eyes, but took the onion Mom handed her.

"Did you make any new friends?"

"Yeah, I guess so. I mean, one girl seems okay."

"Anything . . . else happen?"

Georgie knew Mom wanted to know if she'd seen the guidance counselor. She'd expected to get the third degree when she came home last week with her books. When Mom didn't say anything, Georgie knew that Mom hadn't expected her to be called in so soon. She'd decided then and there that Mom would have to beg before Georgie would tell her that, yes, she had visited the guidance counselor like a good girl.

"Nothing worth mentioning." She gave the onion a good whack, chopping it right in two.

"I swear, Georgia Francine, you are as hardheaded as your daddy."

"Thanks!" Georgie said.

Mom stopped stirring the ground beef in the skillet and put her hands on her hips. "Did you or did you not see the guidance counselor today?"

"Nope," Georgie said.

"No?" Mom looked worried.

Georgie shrugged. "I saw her last week."

"And?"

"And . . . I liked her glasses." Georgie smiled at her own reply.

"You think you're mighty clever, don't you, young lady? Georgie, talking things out can be good for you. I just thought if you didn't want to talk to me, maybe you'd talk to her."

"Okay. Got it. You made a guess and you were wrong." Georgie dumped the chopped onion into the skillet, creating a loud sizzle and rising steam. "I'm going to watch the news. Let me know when this is done."

"Georgie, no! Stay here with me. We don't have to talk, just keep me company."

"Can't." Georgie turned to go.

"It's a clear night; we'll go sky watching instead. I know how much you like that."

Georgie hesitated. She knew she'd eventually go outside to see the moon, but the news wouldn't wait. "We can do that after the news."

She escaped to the living room. Even empty, it held the smell of baby powder. Gagging, Georgie flipped the knob until Walter Cronkite filled the screen.

There was a time when Mom had watched the news with her, as anxious for a sign of Dad as she was. But Mom didn't do that anymore. She either cooked dinner during the news or went for a walk. Well, Georgie wasn't giving up. Tonight might be the night. And she couldn't really get mad at Mom because, in a way, Mom had been short-changed.

Georgie knew Mom needed a different kind of daughter than the one she got. She needed one who helped with the brats. Heck, one who didn't *call* them brats! Mom needed a daughter she could talk to.

But Georgie didn't need anyone to talk to. She didn't need Mom or Mrs. Donovan.

Georgie needed her dad.

Georgie found her seat in social studies. Yesterday she had been happy to see that Lisa was in her class. But Lisa had clearly been too busy looking all dreamy-eyed at Craig Evans to notice Georgie.

Their teacher, Mr. Hennessy, was short, just a little taller than Georgie. Today he was dressed in gray pants and a matching turtleneck. He was totally bald, except for a band of white fringe around the sides and back of his head. That, along with his bushy, white eyebrows and beard, made his head look like a white ring around a ball. He reminded Georgie of a stick of roll-on deodorant.

"Now that we're finished with all the first-day business of working out seating arrangements and whatnot, we can get to the real reason we're here: social studies, or, more accurately, geography." He rocked back and forth from his toes to his heels, as if he had too much energy to stand still.

"Now, you've all learned quite a bit about our country in elementary school, so I won't bore you with more of that. I say, if you want to know what it's like in Schenectady, call your Aunt Mabel!"

The class laughed. Georgie liked this little man.

"The place that's on most of our minds is one that's only a little bigger than New Mexico. The place I'm talking about is, of course, Vietnam."

He picked up some chalk and began to sketch the country on the blackboard. He had it all wrong. His drawing looked like the handset of a phone. Georgie could barely stay in her seat. She wanted to grab his chalk and show him the gentle curve of the Gulf of Tonkin and how the land gradually widened beside Laos. But that would make her a show-off and she knew better.

"Does anyone have family serving there now?" he asked.

Georgie's hand shot high into the air. "My dad," she said.

Kathy Newman, the girl Lisa said was her ex-friend, raised her hand. "My brother is there."

"Yes, I know your brother, Brian." Mr. Hennessy smiled. "We'll be talking about the land, but I think it's important that first we get in a little history lesson, just to make sure we're all clear on why our soldiers are there."

34

Craig said, "If you know that, you should be in the White House."

There were laughs, and two fingers held up in peace signs flashed around the room.

"It does seem to be the question of the decade," Mr. Hennessy agreed. "I'll do what I can to help explain things. You've all grown up hearing about Vietnam, but I can tell you that eight or nine years ago, in the early sixties, very few people even knew where it was. We associate it with an ugly war now, but it once was a small, gorgeous country with thick jungles and lovely white beaches."

Georgie perked up. Her dad was the only other person she'd heard say anything about how beautiful the country could be.

"It was a French colony until the 1950s, so in some ways it's an old country; in others, it's very young. Americans thought it should have a government like ours. It was a divided country, though, with the north ruled by Communists," Mr. Hennessy said. "We had hopes for the south, but it quickly turned into a dictatorship, rather than a democracy. So, being Americans and *always* wanting to help"—he paused and raised his bushy eyebrows to some laughter—"we tried to teach the south, called the Army of the Republic of Vietnam, how to use the weapons that we were so graciously providing."

Mr. Hennessy wrote "1965" on the board. "Can anyone tell me why this year is important?"

Everyone slid down in their seats. Maybe he wasn't going to be such a great teacher after all, asking questions about stupid stuff he hadn't covered yet. Georgie looked at Lisa, but she was writing with her head down.

"It's the first year we were in the war completely. We went in bombing the north, sure to scare them with our impressive army—think John Wayne."

A few kids giggled, but Georgie crossed her arms. Her dad was a pilot and she was steamed. Dad only did what he had to do; he never thought of himself as saving the day like John Wayne.

Mr. Hennessy went on. "But that didn't work. Seemed to make the north madder, if anything. So we went in on foot, and that's not been too successful, either. The Communists from the north, called NVA for North Vietnamese Army, use the jungles and mountains to hide in. They also use their swamps, and they've dug underground tunnels. You see, they know the land. We don't."

Georgie took off her cap. It was hard to listen to, yet fascinating at the same time. Kind of like passing a smashed-up car. You're sick that it happened but can't help taking a peek as you drive by.

"Anyone know another reason why 1965 is important? Besides that I still had a little hair on top?"

"We were only second-graders," Georgie said. "How could we know that?"

"That's true." Mr. Hennessy looked down, probably trying to find her name on his seating chart. "Georgie. It's the year the antiwar movement came out in full swing."

Someone said, "Right on!" Georgie didn't look up to see who'd said it. She knew she'd hate that kid forever and this was only the first week of school. It was too early to start a list of enemies.

Mr. Hennessy said, "I believe it's an injustice to talk about the war without talking about how it has divided our own country. When one hundred thousand people feel strongly enough about something to have demonstrations that lead to riots, well, they can't be ignored, now, can they?"

Several *no*'s were mumbled.

Craig Evans raised his hand. "President Johnson seemed to be able to ignore how the demonstrators feel. And now Nixon's doing it."

"It might seem that way. But politics can cloud common sense sometimes. And we mustn't forget that every argument has two sides."

Craig said, "I know there are people who think we belong there. They should be the ones who go and fight. The draft just isn't right. You shouldn't be forced to fight in a war you don't believe in."

One boy raised his hand. "Hey, my older brother got a low draft number, so my parents made him join the National Guard."

"It's true that a lot of boys don't want to be there," Mr. Hennessy said. "Some join the Guard, hoping they won't be called to fight. Enrollment in our colleges is greater than it would have been without the war, since, as we all know, you don't have to serve if you're in school. And, of course, some young men are leaving our country altogether, even though they would be arrested if caught."

Mr. Hennessy looked at Lisa's hand, which was slightly raised. He consulted his chart and said, "Yes, Lisa?"

"May I use the restroom, Mr. Hennessy?"

Georgie could barely hear her. Lisa's face was pale and she seemed very nervous.

Mr. Hennessy hesitated a minute, then said, "Yes, if you can't wait."

Lisa had already stacked her books. She scooped them up, and slid around the back of the room and out the door. *She must really have to go,* Georgie thought.

Mr. Hennessy went from bouncing in front of the board to pacing the room. "So, you do have a point, Craig. It would be nice if we were able to send just the boys who wanted to fight. But what if not enough people volunteered? It's difficult to win a war that way."

"We don't seem to be doing so hot with the whole country over there," Craig said.

Georgie couldn't hold back any longer. Her hand shot up. "Excuse me, Mr. Hennessy. I must have wandered into the wrong classroom. I'm supposed to be in social studies and here I am studying the Opinions of Craig Evans by mistake."

There was a blast of laughter. Even Mr. Hennessy chuckled. "You are absolutely correct, Georgie. This is social studies. Now, is there anything you'd like to ask me about Vietnam, other than politics, before we move on to another country?"

Georgie leaned back. She felt as if she'd just been given a gift. There was something she very much wanted to know about Vietnam.

"Yes, sir. Could you please tell me more about those places where a person could hide?"

6 Miss Horton passed out yesterday's math homework. Georgie peeked at her grade: 100 percent correct. She wasn't surprised. Getting A's wasn't anything new to Georgie. She'd learned not to announce that she was smart, though. It was part of her survival strategy.

Georgie had been in third grade the first time she switched schools. She'd loved school. She'd loved her old friends and had expected to love new ones.

After the first week, two girls from her class got off at her bus stop. They followed her for a block, calling her names. Georgie was only eight years old at the time. She was scared and walked faster, but one of the girls rushed behind her and pushed her down. They laughed and ran away. Georgie sat on the sidewalk, cradled her bleeding hands, and cried.

That's how her dad found her. He sat beside her, gently wiping first her tears, then her blood, with his handkerchief while she told him how awful the new school was.

"They make fun of me when I give the right answer. If I sit at their table at lunch, they scoot away and whisper so I can't hear. *No one* plays with me at recess."

"Sounds like we need to devise a battle plan, Captain," he said. "A survival strategy."

And that's what they'd done. Georgie let Miss Horton drone on as she remembered how her dad had sat with her at the kitchen table and together they'd written up a plan to help her survive in the new school.

"You say they make fun if you know the right answers," Dad said. "Do you like getting good grades?"

"Yes!" Georgie said. "I like school."

"But no one sits with you at lunch? No one plays with you at recess?"

Georgie bit her bottom lip and shook her head.

"What about these girls from the bus? What did you do when they called you names?"

"I walked faster."

"Well, Captain," Dad said, "we can make up a battle plan, but you have to decide if you're up to the fight. Are you, soldier?"

"Yes, sir!" Georgie saluted.

"That's my girl."

Dad wrote the words *Standing Orders* at the top of the page.

"What are standing orders?" Georgie asked.

"That's what you do no matter what. Since you like to get good grades, your standing orders are to get the best grades you can."

Georgie slunk in her seat. She'd be dead in a week.

"But," Dad said.

"But what?"

"But you don't have to tell anyone what your grades are. That's between you and your teacher. You have your commanding officer's—that's me—you have my permission to fib and say you didn't do so well to the other kids."

Georgie laughed. This was going better than she had hoped.

"Your second standing order is to never let anyone mess with you. If someone picks on you, pick right back. Remember, the enemy smells fear, so you can't let them know you're afraid. You got that, Captain?"

Georgie nodded solemnly.

"Last standing order: don't get cut off from your outfit. That means don't be alone. The best thing is to find a friend. Not a group of friends. Groups tend to turn on themselves. But find one person you like and do things with her."

Georgie thought of the girl who'd shared her colored pencils in art class.

"Yes, sir."

"Fine! Now, for our provisional plan," Dad said. "That's what you do if your first plan fails."

"Okay," Georgie said. "What's that?"

Georgie's dad relaxed in his chair. He pulled her onto his lap and said, "You come tell your commanding officer about it. He'll buy you an ice cream cone and then go have a talk with the enemy's mommy and daddy."

Georgie giggled and threw her arms around his neck.

Mom said, "Bill, for heaven's sake! It's third grade, not a war."

"Guess you're right, darlin'," Dad said. But he folded the paper and slipped it to Georgie with a wink.

Georgie had felt as if all the love she had floated out of her and onto her dad at that moment. He understood her better than anyone, and his battle plan was perfect. She had used it at every school.

"Class, turn to page eleven, please," Miss Horton said, pulling Georgie's thoughts back.

Georgie looked at Lisa. She had a good feeling about her. Lisa seemed nice, but wasn't afraid to go along with Georgie on rebelling against that stupid Good Deeds program. And spying on her family at the town picnic showed she wasn't dull. It wasn't too hard finding a friend, but it *was* hard finding one who wasn't boring.

Lisa hurried toward Georgie as soon as the bell rang.

"Hi, Georgie!" she called. "I hate math, don't you?"

"Can't stand it," Georgie said.

"I got an eighty-five on yesterday's homework. That's pretty good for me. What did you get?"

"Seventy," Georgie lied.

"Oh, well," Lisa said. "Don't feel bad. It's so hard!"

"No kidding." Georgie grabbed her science book from her locker and then walked with Lisa to hers.

Lisa picked up her English book. They had their first classes, social studies and math, together, so they'd gotten into the habit of walking to each other's lockers.

"Okay, ready." Lisa turned just as Craig walked up to her. "Hi, Craig," she said, and her face flushed.

Georgie looked at Craig. She didn't want to hate him, but it was hard not to. He'd made it clear he thought the war was wrong. She wanted it to end, too, but honorably.

"Hi, Lisa." He looked at Georgie as if he wanted her to go away.

When she didn't move, he cleared his throat and said to Lisa, "I was, um, wondering if you had a partner for the Good Deeds thing."

"Oh!" Lisa said.

Georgie asked, "Why do you want to know?"

"Well—um—"

Putting him on the spot felt good.

"I signed up for the Keep America Beautiful project," he said. "I heard the assignment will be to plant trees, and I thought being outside would be kind of nice." He looked down at his shoes. "And, well, since we're from different sides of town now, I thought if you didn't have a partner . . ."

"Well . . . I *do* have a partner," Lisa said. "But—I—" She looked to Georgie for help.

Georgie smiled at her but didn't say anything. She loved watching the two of them squirm. She felt back in control.

"Well, that's good that you have a partner. I guess I'd better find one, too," he said. "Nice talking to you."

He walked away. Lisa groaned and banged her head on her locker door.

"Why are you doing that?" Georgie said.

"Are you blind? Don't you think he's the cutest guy in the whole school? He used to be in my class, but his parents moved across town to Glendale. The best part about Glendale and North Ridge consolidating is that we're in the same school again, but every single time he talks to me, I stammer."

"He seems to have the same problem," Georgie said. "You should have told him your partner was Ringo."

"So then he thinks I'm an idiot? No, thanks."

"He might have gotten that impression anyway," Georgie said.

Lisa looked so stricken that Georgie burst out laughing. "I'm kidding!" She gave Lisa a shove.

Lisa laughed a little. Then the bell rang and she let out a squeal. She ran in the direction of her English class, while Georgie slowly sauntered toward her science lab.

As soon as Principal Gordon finished announcements Friday morning, the school secretary, Mrs. Sanders, came back on the intercom. "Would Lisa Loutzenhiser and Georgia Collins report to the principal's office, please."

Georgie's first thought was that it must be payback time for destroying Mrs. Donovan's ship. But not if Lisa was called in, too, she realized.

Lisa quickly gathered her books and almost ran toward the office.

"What's your hurry?" Georgie said as she followed her.

"I wonder if something bad happened at home."

"Why would you think that?"

"Why else would we get called to the office?"

"You've never been sent to the principal's office for getting into trouble?" Georgie asked.

"Of course not!" Lisa looked so innocent, like a chicken right before its neck is wrung.

Mrs. Sanders was busy on the phone. Too bad. Georgie remembered her from the week before school started. She'd enjoy giving Mrs. Sanders a hard time again. Some people were such easy targets. Instead, Georgie sat in a chair and picked up a pamphlet: *How to Get the Most out of Your Education.* "This should be good for a laugh," she said.

Lisa stood at the reception desk and tried to catch her breath.

"Hello, Lisa."

Georgie looked up to see Kathy Newman coming out of the supply room.

"Hi!" Lisa said. "Were you called to the office, too?"

"Me? No. I volunteer here during homeroom," Kathy said.

"Oh, that's nice."

Kathy seemed kind of friendly. Lisa must have exaggerated when she said they weren't friends anymore. Or maybe they had made up. Georgie went back to her pamphlet. Then she noticed that Kathy and Lisa were arguing. She loved a good fight, so she tossed the pamphlet down.

"How can you be so stupid, Lisa?" Kathy asked.

"I thought we could put all that behind us," Lisa whined. She looked as pathetic as a dog left out in the rain. Georgie made a mental note to work on that with Lisa. Never appear weak to the enemy.

"Yeah, well, that's easier for you than me," Kathy said.

At that moment, Mrs. Sanders hung up the phone and turned to Lisa. "May I help you?"

"I'm Lisa Loutzenhiser. I was called to the office."

"Oh, you're here to see the principal! Didn't Kathy tell you?"

Before Lisa could answer, Kathy said, "Yes, Mrs. Sanders. I told her that Principal Gordon is expecting her and that other girl." Then she said to Lisa, "I doubt he'll be in a good mood, since you've kept him waiting. I'll have to tell him how you wouldn't stop gabbing."

"But—I—" Lisa's face was all splotchy. "You didn't tell me!"

"Sure I did, Lisa," Kathy lied. "I told you as soon as you walked in the door."

Georgie followed Lisa into the office. She didn't know what was going on with those two, but it would be fun finding out.

Principal Gordon sat back and looked at the girls. He took off his glasses, chewed an earpiece, then put them back on.

"It was nice of you to finally join me, ladies."

Lisa said, "I'm sorry we're late, we didn't—"

Mr. Gordon held up his hand. "Not now, please."

The room was silent except for the sound of the clock's ticking. Mr. Gordon was in no hurry. Georgie examined her fingernails. Lisa squirmed in her seat. Georgie was really going to have to give Lisa lessons on handling pressure.

Finally, Mr. Gordon picked up a stack of papers, shuffled them, and cleared his throat. "Tell me, Lisa, how is Richard Starkey these days?"

So, that's all it was! Georgie relaxed, but Lisa pressed on the inside corners of her eyes, as if to keep from crying.

"And Georgie's partner is Simon Garfunkel." Mr. Gordon leaned back. "Ladies, if you had done your homework, you'd know I'm a Beatles fan. Nice touch using Ringo Starr's real name, though. Richard Starkey is such a com-

47

mon name, it might have gone unnoticed. But Simon Garfunkel? Really."

"Next time we'll try to be a little more creative,"
Georgie said.

"Good idea," Mr. Gordon said. "So, girls, how did we
do? Is this the first test you've put our little school
through?"

"Yeah. It's the first," Georgie said. "You get an A."

"That's good to know. It looks as if you two will have
to be partners after all, since everyone else already has one."
He looked at them over the top of his glasses. "You've already proven that you work well together. However, by
pulling your prank, you lose your choice of projects.
They've all been taken except one. You win it by default."

"I can't wait to hear what it is," Georgie said.

"It's a request from the staff at the Sunset Home for the
Aged."

Mr. Gordon slipped a letter from an envelope and read:
"'Mrs. Sophia Albertson is a lovely lady who rarely gets visitors. When we heard about your Good Deeds program, we
thought it would be a wonderful opportunity for Sophia to
have guests.'"

He stopped reading and Georgie groaned. "An old
folks' home? You've got to be kidding!"

"Shhh," Lisa whispered.

"Well, have you ever been to one?" Georgie asked.
"They stink to high heaven. People use bedpans and grown
men and women wear diapers."

She looked at Mr. Gordon. "Hey, we don't have to empty bedpans, right? Because I'll take an F before I'll touch one of those."

Mr. Gordon lowered his voice. "Don't push me, Georgie. My hunch is that, for whatever reason, you wanted to get caught. You seem too clever to set yourself up like this. So I'll play along for now. You're in the principal's office and you've established yourself as a troublemaker."

Lisa's head jerked up. "You didn't want to get into trouble, did you?"

Georgie shrugged.

"Oh!" Lisa cried out.

Maybe it wasn't her best idea ever, but Georgie hadn't exactly wanted to get caught. Had she?

"Georgie, how could you?" Lisa said.

"You don't have to be such a baby about it."

"Girls!" Mr. Gordon leaned back in his chair. "You'll visit Mrs. Albertson Saturday morning—tomorrow—at ten o'clock. The staff is expecting you, and we'll check to make sure you visit at least once a week. I know you'll be there for the next six Saturdays. Right, Lisa?"

Lisa nodded vigorously. Sure she would. Georgie would have bet that Lisa would mop his floor with her hair to gain back her good-girl status.

"Right, Georgie?"

Georgie smiled her fake smile. "Right, Mr. Gordon."

* * *

Georgie had just turned her book to the correct page in math class when there was a knock at the door.

"Come in," Miss Horton called. Mrs. Donovan walked over to her desk and whispered something to her.

"Georgie? Bring your things, please." Miss Horton jotted down the day's assignments for her and said, "You're to go with Mrs. Donovan now."

Georgie expected to get busted for destroying Mrs. Donovan's ship, but did it have to be today? She had already been called into the office once. She snatched the paper out of Miss Horton's hand and stomped down the hall behind Mrs. Donovan.

When Georgie stepped into the office, Mrs. Sanders wore a superior look on her face, as if she knew Georgie was in trouble. Georgie raised her head high. She wasn't about to let on that what Mrs. Sanders thought bothered her. Not one bit.

This time Mrs. Donovan sat but didn't say anything, so Georgie sat across from her in the circle of chairs. Georgie glanced at the shelf where the boat bottle had been. It was empty, but the spotlight was still on. To make her feel guilty, she supposed. Georgie crossed her arms and waited. Well, it wouldn't work.

"I'm sorry I pulled you out of class," Mrs. Donovan said.

"Then don't."

Mrs. Donovan blinked. "Don't what?"

"Don't pull me out," Georgie said.

"I realize you don't want to be here, Georgie, but I feel it's important. Your mother feels so, too."

"And what I want doesn't count?"

"Of course it does," Mrs. Donovan said. "But what we want and what we need aren't always the same thing."

"Listen, you don't even know me, so you can't know what I need."

"Do you think your mother knows what you need, Georgie?" Mrs. Donovan asked in a low voice.

The room was so stuffy that Georgie pulled on her collar. She could barely breathe. Mrs. Donovan sat there, cool as an early spring day, while Georgie felt as if she would suffocate.

"It's hot in here," Georgie said.

"I don't think so. Maybe you're feeling uncomfortable because of my question. I asked if you think your mother knows what you need."

It made Georgie want to hurt her again. She pushed one of the chairs aside and went to the shelves. She swished her hand around the empty spot. "Looks like what *you* need is a bottle here."

Georgie felt some satisfaction at the look on Mrs. Donovan's face.

"Is that remark meant to wound me?" Mrs. Donovan asked.

"Well, I know you can't be happy about it. And we both know I did it," Georgie said. "Let's just get to the part where I'm in trouble. What will it be? Detention?"

"I don't want to put you in detention. You were angry and acted out. It's not the first thing that's been broken in my office."

"But it meant a lot to you," Georgie said. What was with this woman? Georgie almost felt as if it was her job to get into trouble now.

"It was just a thing. Things aren't that important to me. People are. Like you," Mrs. Donovan said.

"Oh, pul-eeze," Georgie groaned. "That sensitive, caring crap is worse than Chinese water torture."

"Okay, I'll stop talking," Mrs. Donovan said. "But only if you start."

"Fine, what do you want to talk about? What it's like to be in seventh grade? What it's like to be a new student here? Oh, wait! I know. How about what it's like to be forced to talk to you?"

"Why don't you tell me what it's been like having a father in Vietnam?"

"It's great. He sends home all the rice we can eat. The only thing I hate is that he doesn't have to pay postage on his letters. I'd really hoped to add to my stamp collection."

"You sound angry."

"I do? And I was going for funny," Georgie said. "I guess I'll have to work on my timing."

Mrs. Donovan looked at Georgie. Georgie stared back. Finally Mrs. Donovan said, "So, you regret that he didn't help with your stamp collection. Is that the only feeling you've experienced regarding your father's last Vietnam tour?"

"That's right," Georgie said.

Mrs. Donovan said, "You must miss him very much."

"Well, it's not like he can come home for supper when he's in the middle of a war."

"War could keep him away," Mrs. Donovan said. "Among other things."

"What's that supposed to mean?" Georgie asked.

"As I said earlier, Georgie, your mother and I have talked."

Georgie had made a mistake letting Mrs. Donovan get to her. She began staring at Mrs. Donovan's glasses again and let her rattle on. Georgie tried to bring back the memory she had earlier of her dad writing out her battle plan. She could see him running his left hand through his hair as he wrote. The memory made her feel calm and safe.

"It looks as if we're not gaining much ground today, are we?" Mrs. Donovan said. "I'll let you go back to class."

She picked up Georgie's books and handed them to her. "I wouldn't want you to have to come back for them." She gave a small smile.

Georgie ignored the remark and grabbed the books.

"Oh, Georgie," Mrs. Donovan said, "just so you know, I'll pull you from class again from time to time. To talk more."

"Great. Just make sure it's during home ec." Georgie opened the door. "I stink at cooking."

8 Georgie looked at her bedroom clock. Lisa would just be getting off the bus at the corner of Fifth and Pine Street. They had agreed to meet there at nine-thirty Saturday morning, then walk together to the Sunset Home.

Georgie was still annoyed about the way Lisa had acted in Mr. Gordon's office and afterward. "Oh, you don't think they'll call our parents, do you, Georgie? I'll just *die* if they call my dad!" Georgie hoped they *would* call if Lisa was going to be such a crybaby about it.

Georgie threw on her granny sunglasses and a huge hat like the ones people wear on safaris. She didn't even brush her hair. The bus stop was a short distance from her house, so she took her time walking there.

When she saw Lisa anxiously pacing at the bus stop, with a wide-eyed, worried look, Georgie felt even more annoyed.

"Georgie! I've been waiting for ten minutes. I'm so glad you're here."

"Let's get this over with" was the only greeting Georgie gave Lisa.

"Are you mad?" Lisa asked.

"We're working for free at an old folks' home, Lisa. I should act happy?"

"But we could've had our pick of projects if we hadn't played that trick!" Lisa said.

Georgie looked over the top of her sunglasses. "Has anyone ever told you how irritating you are when you whine?"

Lisa sucked in her breath. They walked in silence until they came to the sign that said SUNSET HOME FOR THE AGED.

"I don't think it's a nursing home, Georgie. It looks more like a retirement home or a place where you go when you need a little help taking care of yourself."

"That probably means they clean out their own bedpans." Georgie snorted. "Some improvement."

"The place must have been pretty at one time, don't you think?" asked Lisa. "I mean, those tall peaks might look kind of like princess towers if you were a little kid."

Georgie looked and she knew what Lisa meant. The main part of the building probably had been a stately house at one time, but one-story modern wings had been added to each side. They didn't go together at all.

"Yeah," Georgie said. "But now it looks kinda bizarre. Which is a heck of a lot better than pretty, if you ask me."

"I don't think *bizarre* is the right word. Disrespectful, maybe."

"Disrespectful!" Georgie said. "To a building?" She chuckled. "I'll bet you're a writer, aren't you? One of those artsy people?"

Lisa looked at Georgie so fast and with such a stricken face that Georgie almost felt bad. She took off the safari hat, scratched her head, and crammed the hat back down on her hair. "Oh, forget it. It was just a guess. Besides, everybody has their quirks."

When Lisa didn't say anything, Georgie said, "Just ring the doorbell. Maybe we'll get lucky and no one will answer."

"They have a staff. Someone will answer." Lisa pushed the button.

The door was slowly opened by a woman wearing a faded red dress that had to be from the 1940s. It had huge shoulder pads and a skirt that hung past the woman's knees. She wore a tight-fitting green hat with flowers all around it. Her hair was tucked up inside, but one very long gray strand escaped down the back.

"Good morning, girls," she said. "Won't you come in?"

They stepped into the cool foyer. It took a few minutes to get used to the darkness after the sunlight.

Lisa said, "Hello, I'm Lisa Loutzenhiser."

"Loutzenhiser! What an unusual name."

"It's Italian," Georgie said as she lifted the lid of an urn on the hall table.

"And this is Georgia Collins," Lisa said.

Leave it to Lisa to remember her manners. Georgie peered into the urn.

"I see you've met Madge." The woman waved her hand toward the urn. "She was a resident here. After she passed on, we decided to put her ashes in the entryway. Madge always loved it when company came to the door."

Georgie dropped the lid so fast it clanked. She immediately recovered from the shock and said, "Far out!"

"Follow me," the lady ordered.

Lisa started to follow, but Georgie pulled on the back of her shirt. She grabbed a used ashtray off the hall table and held it up for Lisa to see.

"Who do you suppose this was? Madge's husband?"

It was funny. How could Lisa not laugh? Instead she said, "Why don't you knock it off? Let's just be normal, all right?"

Georgie let go of Lisa's shirt as if it were on fire. "What's with you?"

"I just don't want to act stupid or goofy while we're here, that's all. What's wrong with that?"

There was plenty wrong with that. And plenty wrong with Lisa, too. Georgie sailed past her into the reception room.

"Georgie?" Lisa said.

Georgie ignored her.

"Now, what can I do for you girls?" the lady said.

"Um, we're from Glendale Middle School," Lisa said.

"And?"

"We came to visit Mrs. Albertson."

A side door creaked open and a large woman came in. Her caramel-colored skin contrasted with the white uniform she wore. "Aggy?" she said. "What are you doin'?"

The woman in the 1940s dress said in a childlike voice,

57

"I was just playing, Camille. I was pretending to be the lady of the manor."

"You know playin' is one thing. But you answer that door, you're supposed to be yourself," the woman named Camille said. Aggy hung her head.

"So, you're the girls from the school?" Camille said. Lisa nodded.

"Aggy, you run on and tell Sophia she's got company."

Aggy smiled so widely that her eyes turned into slits. "Okay!" She wobbled out of the room on her high heels.

"I'm Camille. I'm one of the nurse's aides here," she said. "I can't tell you how tickled Sophia's gonna be to have company." She said the word *company* as if it had no *a*—*comp'ny*. Her soft Southern accent reminded Georgie of her dad, and, despite herself, she felt her insides warm a little.

"Your school sent us a sign-in paper. Let me get it." Camille rummaged through a drawer at the front desk. "Here we go. A letter came with it that said you were supposed to visit for two hours every week for six weeks."

Lisa picked up the pen and filled out her line. She handed the pen to Georgie.

Georgie shook her head in disbelief.

"Come on, Georgie," Lisa said. "I'm sure all the students have to do this."

Georgie practically ripped the pen from Lisa's hand. "I don't like this. It's like they're spying on us or something." She quickly signed and left Lisa to fill in the date and time for her.

58

Camille said, "Good, good. Now, come on. I'll take you to meet Sophia. You're just gonna love her. We all do."

Lisa went through the door, but Georgie didn't move. Camille stopped and put her hands on her hips. "Come on, child. I ain't got all day and wouldn't want to waste it here if I did." She stood in the doorway.

Georgie thought of leaving, but something about Camille's don't-argue-with-me attitude made Georgie slowly shuffle past her.

In the parlor Georgie saw an old gentleman carrying a box of checkers into a room. He walked with a cane. She saw two old women watching television. One of them was knitting.

"This is a nice place, Camille," Lisa said. "You have so many homey touches, like the braided rugs on the floor and the doilies."

"We try to make it as much like home as we can."

Georgie couldn't help herself. "And don't forget that nice *homey* antiseptic smell." She snorted. "If you ask me, keeping a dead person's ashes doesn't sound too much like home."

Camille stopped and stared down at Georgie. "And what are you talkin' about?"

"That Aggy. She said Madge used to live here and now her ashes are in the urn by the front door."

"I think Aggy's been watching that soap opera *Dark Shadows* again. Most of what she says comes from television." Camille's expression didn't change. "We've never had a Madge, dead or alive. And you'd think a person who looks as smart as you would recognize salt when she sees it."

"Salt?"

"For when the walk gets icy in the winter. We can't be havin' our residents fallin' on ice. Half of them can't walk good as it is."

Camille stopped at room 17 and said, "You girls go on to the sitting room at the end of the hall. I'll bring Sophia down directly."

Georgie flopped into a chair in the sitting room.

"It's not a bad place, don't you think?" Lisa asked.

Before Georgie could answer, Camille wheeled Sophia into the room.

"I'll leave you all here for a little visit," Camille said. "We'll have treats after you get acquainted."

Sophia sat in her wheelchair, a colorful afghan over her knees. She was thin, with wavy silver hair. Her face had a natural look of worry, as if the lines on it were etched that way permanently, even when she smiled at the girls.

"Hello, I'm Sophia Albertson. I'm sorry, but I don't know who you are."

"I'm Lisa!" She was quick to answer. "Lisa Loutzenhiser, Mrs. Albertson, and this is Georgie Collins."

Georgie ignored them and pretended to study a picture.

"Loutzenhiser, that's—"

"Polish," Georgie interrupted. "It means two-headed freak."

Lisa's face went white.

"Really? I was about to say that it's an old German name. One I haven't heard in quite some time." She looked confused. "It's Polish, you say?"

Lisa said, "Georgie's just kidding around."

"I see." Sophia brightened a little. "Well, I'm pleased to meet you both. Now I need you to do two favors for me. Please call me Sophia. Mrs. Albertson was my mother-in-law. The other favor is, could you please tell me why you're visiting me today? My memory isn't as sharp as it used to be."

Georgie said, "We're here because if we don't do something nice for the community, we flunk. So it's either visit you or get an F."

Sophia's face looked shocked for a second and then sort of closed up, the way leaves protect a flower.

"It's not like that, Sophia!" Lisa said. "It's true that our school has a program to help the community, but we had choices. Lots of them! We thought you sounded like such a nice lady that we wanted to visit you."

Georgie had to give Lisa credit for lying well when she had to, but it was too late. Sophia said, "I see. Well, now you've done your duty. You can tell your teacher you did your job. I don't know how you got my name, but I'm certainly in no need of visitors."

Sophia unlatched the brake on her wheelchair and said, "Good day."

As she watched Sophia wheel toward the door, Georgie

thought, *Good riddance.* If Sophia didn't want them to visit, Mr. Gordon couldn't make them.

Suddenly Aggy burst into the room. Her faded gray hair hung about her face and she had changed into a caftan that billowed around her bare feet. She looked like an old hippie.

"It's brunch!" Aggy called.

"Aggy, the girls were just leaving," Sophia said.

"Not now. We get to eat and I set the table!"

She grabbed the wheelchair handle and took off at a dead run. Sophia squeezed the armrests so tight her knuckles turned white. Aggy called out, "Faster than a speeding bullet. More powerful than a locomotive. Able to leap tall buildings in a single bound . . ."

She skidded the wheelchair around a corner and they were out of sight.

Georgie headed for the front door.

Lisa said, "The dining room is this way."

"I know," Georgie said. "Which is why I'm going the other way. She said she doesn't want us to visit so I'm leaving. This is our ticket out."

"Okay, fine. We won't come back, but we're here now and it would be rude to just leave. Please, Georgie."

"I don't want to have *brunch*, okay? Even the word is stupid. It's something square people do. You stay, Lisa. You'll fit right in."

Georgie was losing her cool fast. She'd been holding her breath, breathing only when she had to because she thought the place stank. It didn't matter that the people seemed clean and able to get themselves to the restroom. Georgie *still* thought of dirty diapers and drool. Now they expected her to eat.

Georgie thought of how Sophia had sat so regally in that wheelchair, almost as if it were a throne. Didn't she know how pathetic she looked? Aggy might actually be fun, in a creepy sort of way. But Georgie couldn't like any of it after Lisa had bitten her head off.

I just don't want to act stupid or goofy, she'd said. *Let's just be normal, all right?* "Let's just be *boring*. Let's just be *fake*," she might as well have said.

Georgie definitely wanted to leave, but the feeling that her body wasn't big enough to hold all her anger came over her. It had been happening more and more lately. Suddenly she didn't want to go—not because she wanted to stay, but because she wanted them to feel as lousy as she did.

She walked toward the dining room. "I'll stay, but just remember, you asked for this."

Georgie sat, putting her feet up on an empty chair as she watched Aggy pour tea into mismatched teacups. It was as if she were having a kids' tea party with her mom's castoffs. Sophia smiled her thanks when Aggy passed a paper napkin to her. The napkin Aggy put in front of Georgie said "Happy Birthday." Georgie watched Lisa lay her heart-shaped napkin with "Be Mine" in pink letters on her lap, cross her ankles, and say, "Yes, please," when Sophia asked if she wanted sugar.

Lisa wasn't the person Georgie had thought she was. Today she was so *perfect*, so *prissy*. She probably walked around with a book on her head and took classes on which fork to use and stupid etiquette junk like that. She'd been whiny ever since Mr. Gordon had called them in. And now she was simpering over a dumb piece of crumb cake. Georgie decided she didn't like Lisa at all.

"There!" Aggy said after everyone had been served. She sat in the tall chair, her back not quite touching it. She drank her tea with her pinkie stuck out. She smiled at Georgie, and little fans of wrinkles appeared at the corners of her eyes.

Georgie wanted to barf. The air was stuffy. She was sure she would smell the place for days after she left. Aggy was crazy as a loon and Lisa behaved as if she were having tea with the Queen of England instead of the Mad Hatter.

Georgie looked around the room. Lisa would pay for making her feel so angry. She saw the old man with the cane hobble into the room. She could trip him, she thought. Lisa would hate her, but they'd kick Georgie out of there and she wouldn't have to go back.

But Georgie couldn't make herself hurt an old man.

Just then, Georgie noticed Aggy leaning to the side. Suddenly there was a loud *pplllllllllllooofff!*

"What was *that*?" Georgie asked.

Sophia finished sipping her tea and put the cup back on its saucer. "Well, Georgie, I do believe Aggy sat on a duck."

Aggy beamed as if she'd blessed them all with a gift and sang out the Alka-Seltzer jingle: "Plop, plop, fizz, fizz, oh, what a relief it is!"

Georgie quickly looked at Lisa, who lifted her head up, startled. Her lips parted and splashes of pink sprang up on her cheeks, as if she'd never before heard a fart outside a bathroom.

Georgie cackled. She laughed so hard that she slid out of her seat onto the floor.

She held her side, gasping for breath, and looked up at Lisa. Lisa stared at her for a minute and then laughed. Soon Sophia joined in, and they were lost in a fit of giggles.

When she finally stopped laughing, Georgie was flat on the floor, her anger gone. She wiped tears of laughter from her face and said, "Soph, you've *gotta* let us come back."

Sophia looked down at her hands folded neatly in her lap. "I guess it would be all right. But only if you both want to."

"You really want to, Georgie?" Lisa sounded surprised.

Georgie got up, grabbed a piece of crumb cake, and said, "I wouldn't miss it."

9 Georgie ran into the restroom before lunch on Monday and saw Lisa at the sink.

"Look at this mess!" Lisa said.

Georgie squinted at Lisa's hair. It had a streak of green running down the side.

"You look like Lily on *The Munsters*. Except hers is white," Georgie said, washing her hands.

Lisa moaned and rubbed soap onto her hair.

"What happened anyway?"

"Kathy Newman's in my health class and I heard her telling her new best friend, Angel Cameron, how cute she thought Craig Evans was. I know she was just doing it because I told her last year that I liked him." Lisa turned to the mirror. "We were making posters and I have this stupid habit of tucking my hair behind my ears when I'm nervous. The next thing I knew, I pulled my hair back *and I had green paint on my hand!*"

"It could be worse," Georgie said. "You look good in green."

Lisa flipped water at Georgie for an answer.

Georgie laughed. She'd been so put out with Lisa at the Sunset Home, but by the time they left, she'd decided that Lisa wasn't so bad. She had been looking for her when she came into the restroom.

"You got much homework?" Georgie asked.

"No," Lisa answered. "Not yet anyway. How about you?"

"Nah. Let's do something tonight."

"Tonight?" Lisa asked. "A school night?"

"I can't stand it at my house! My mom has two cribs in the living room for babysitting. Two! I feel like the rooms shrink when I'm there." Georgie yanked a paper towel and dried her hands. "I'd rather go to your house. Better yet, let's go to the Sunset Home. Sophia's a square but Aggy's groovy. I want to see what else she does. It's like a free freak show, y'know?"

Lisa flinched visibly. "Aggy *is* pretty weird, but maybe she can't help it. I mean, she is *old*."

"So?" Georgie said.

"I just don't think we should make fun of her," Lisa said. "Besides, Sophia isn't expecting us until Saturday."

Lisa wiped her hands on a paper towel and then wrapped it around the handle of the bathroom door when she opened it.

Georgie didn't move. "What are you *doing*?"

Lisa looked down at the paper towel. "I'm opening the door. A lot of people don't wash their hands after using the restroom, so I always do this to keep from getting their bacteria."

Georgie threw back her head and laughed.

Lisa's face went straight to red. "Why is that funny?"

"Never mind. You're just different," Georgie said as she walked through the doorway. "If we're not going to the

Sunset *asylum*, I guess that leaves your house. I can be there around seven o'clock."

Georgie scraped the food off a plate, grabbed the dishrag, and began scrubbing before the sink filled with water.

Mom added their dirty silverware to the suds. "I know you're anxious to visit Lisa, but you don't have to be in that big a rush."

"I told her I'd be there at seven. I don't want to miss the news."

"Georgie, not tonight."

"But—"

"No buts." Mom dried her hands. "I said I'd take you to Lisa's, even though this is a school night, because I want you to have fun. You can pay me back by not watching the news."

Georgie threw her dishrag into the sink, spraying bubbles onto the counter. "Fine! I'll call Lisa and tell her I'm not coming."

"You'll do no such thing. I swear, Georgie, if you don't stop this obsession of watching that war play out on television, I'll sell it. And wipe that scowl off your face, young lady."

Georgie knew Mom wouldn't really sell the television, but she felt as if she'd explode if she didn't get out of the house soon. So without another word she fished the dishrag out of the water and attacked a pan.

Mom slowed the station wagon in front of Lisa's house. Georgie opened the door before it had completely stopped.

"Georgia Francine! Don't ever do that again! You could have fallen out."

"Okay. Sorry." She looked at Mom. Georgie used to want to be little again and to curl up on Mom's soft lap. But more and more, she felt that she would suffocate if she didn't get away from her.

"Lisa's a new friend and I like her. I'm just anxious to see her, that's all."

Mom glanced at Lisa's house. "I think I'll come in and meet her mother."

"No!" Georgie almost shouted. "I mean, geez, Mom, talk about embarrassing! You act like I'm a little kid."

"Okay, okay. I can take a hint when I'm clubbed with it." Mom leaned over and hugged Georgie. Georgie didn't shrink away, but she didn't hug back, either.

"Have fun. I'll be here at nine o'clock."

"Right." Georgie threw open the door, slammed it, then immediately felt guilty for not being nicer. She looked at her mother. "See ya at nine." Then she bounded up the steps just as Lisa opened the door.

"Hi!" Lisa said, all smiles.

"Hi."

"Is that your mom?" Lisa asked as the car pulled away.

"Uh-huh."

"I'd like to meet her."

Georgie shrugged. "When you've seen one mom, you've seen them all. So where's your room?"

"Oh, follow me."

They walked through the living room and past the den. Georgie could see Lisa's dad's outline in his chair. The television was throwing odd shadows across the room.

"Is that your dad?" Georgie asked.

"Yeah, but if you've seen one dad, you've seen them all," Lisa said, and laughed.

"That's an easy thing to say when your dad's in the next room, not halfway across the planet," Georgie said.

Lisa pulled her hair behind her ears. Georgie hadn't meant to make her feel bad. Sometimes thoughts seemed to fly out of her mouth by themselves.

"Well, come on. Where's this room?" she said.

Georgie followed Lisa up the stairway, looking at the pictures on the wall as she went. She passed a framed school picture of Denny at the bottom, then Lisa. Next there was the girl Georgie had seen at the picnic, Carla. Near the top was a bare nail with the outline of a picture frame that was no longer there.

"What happened to this picture?' she asked.

Lisa looked at the spot. "Oh, that." She tucked her hair back. "Alan's picture was there. I guess Ma's cleaning the frame or something."

"Where is this Alan anyway?"

"Um, he's—he doesn't live here anymore."

"I know. So where does he live?" Georgie didn't really

care, but Lisa acted so fidgety, it made Georgie push on. "I mean, you mention him but he's never around. He's like a mystery man."

Lisa let out a tiny, high-pitched laugh. "Like *Mystery Date*. Have you ever played that game?"

"Not hardly," Georgie said.

"It's fun! We should do that sometime."

They'd gotten to the top of the stairs when Lisa's little brother opened his door. He held a peanut butter and jelly sandwich in his hand.

"Hey, stickpin!" he said to Lisa.

When she looked his way, he opened his mouth to show the chewed-up food inside.

"Oh, grow up!" Lisa said.

Georgie laughed. He turned to her and nearly choked.

"I know you," she said.

His face turned red and he quickly slammed the door.

Lisa walked into her bedroom. "Denny acts tough around me, but he always clams up when another girl is around. Maybe you should move in."

"Why does he call you stickpin?"

"He says it's because I'm so skinny." Lisa sat on the edge of her bed.

"So is he!" Georgie said.

"Tell him that, will ya."

A plastic beaded curtain divided the room down the center. Georgie grabbed a handful. "Neat-o!"

She moved to the other bed and pushed down, testing for softness. "Whose bed is this?"

"Carla's. She's away at college."

Georgie picked up each stuffed animal that Carla still kept on her shelf. Then she turned around and saw newspaper articles tacked to the wall that read, "Kent Tragedy Was 'Sickening'" and "Stung by the shooting deaths of four Kent State University students, young persons on college campuses across the nation have begun new protests, strikes, and demonstrations against U.S. involvement in Indochina."

Lisa said, "Um, when that happened last May, Carla kind of got involved in the peace movement."

"Yeah, I see." Georgie knew about the students being shot by National Guardsmen during their antiwar protest, but how could she feel sorry for them? For all she knew, her dad was being shot at every day.

"She's not, you know, one of those people who are angry at the soldiers or anything." Lisa sat tall on her bed and held on to a stuffed rabbit. "I mean, she told me about this soldier who came on campus to surprise his girlfriend. Some guys beat him up just 'cause he wore a uniform. She thought that was wrong."

Georgie looked at Lisa out of the corner of her eye. "Am I supposed to be impressed?"

"Well, no, I didn't mean that." Lisa did that hair-behind-the-ears thing again. "I just mean, I know it's probably hard having a dad fighting in Vietnam, then coming

72

here and seeing those pictures. But Carla just wants it all to be over."

Georgie tried to shrug it off. "Who doesn't want that, right?"

Lisa lay back on the bed and hugged the rabbit. "Our dad is pretty ticked off at her. He hasn't stopped paying for her education yet, but he keeps threatening to. And he won't let her come home until she *gets a different attitude.*" Lisa said those words in a deep voice.

Georgie chuckled.

"So there's a lot of tension around here. You might be sorry you came."

"You don't have any babies," Georgie said as she made her way to Lisa's side of the room. "That's a plus."

"I have Denny," Lisa said. "That's a minus."

"What do you normally do when you have a friend over?" Georgie asked.

"I don't know. Same stuff you do, I guess."

"I don't have friends over. We've moved so much I could probably say I don't have friends *period*. That makes you a first, Loutzenhiser."

"You'd better be more specific. You're in a house full of Loutzenhisers," Lisa said. "You know—a house full of two-headed Polish freaks."

Georgie said, "Okay. You got me. I shouldn't have called you that."

"I shouldn't have made you mad. I didn't mean to."

Georgie waved the apology away and sat down next to

73

Lisa and rested her back against the headboard. "I'm serious. What do you do for fun?"

Lisa sat up straight. "Well, when Kathy Newman came over, we'd paint each other's nails and talk about boys. Kathy has this major crush on Donny Osmond, but I think his teeth are huge. And we did each other's hair."

Georgie moved to the dresser so she could look in the mirror. "That one's out. I gave up on my hair a long time ago." She grabbed two handfuls of the bushy stuff.

"No, you've got great hair! Let me show you," Lisa said, joining her. She sectioned off Georgie's hair and braided it while Georgie went through a box of chokers that Lisa kept on her dresser.

Georgie held up one with a cameo on a ribbon and tied it around her neck. "Whoever thought up this dumb idea?"

"I like chokers. That looks good on you."

Georgie turned her head from left to right. "Nah. A chain might be good. Or a dog collar, maybe." She barked like a dog. Lisa laughed and spun Georgie around. Her hair did look kind of nice, with thin braids on the sides gathered into a barrette in the back. But Georgie felt as if she were playing dress-up. It just wasn't her. She wrinkled her nose. "Now I know why I haven't done the girlfriend thing."

"You do mine." Lisa sat down in the chair.

Georgie pulled Lisa's hair straight up on her head. "Do you have a bone I can use, Pebbles?"

Lisa giggled. "Maybe this isn't such a good idea."

74

Georgie continued walking around the room, picking up things as she went. "I can't talk boyfriends with you, either. I think Donny Osmond has big teeth *and* a girlie voice. Not to mention I hate that crappy bubble-gum music."

"We don't have to do the same stuff."

"Let's tell ghost stories!"

"Ghost stories? Isn't that kind of . . . babyish?"

"Okay, let me think. I know, let's tell secrets!"

"I don't think so," Lisa said.

"Come on! I told you one of my deep, dark secrets. I've never done girlfriend things before. What's yours?"

"Um . . ." Lisa began shaking her head. "I don't, you know."

"*I don't, you know* what?" Georgie said.

"I mean, if something is a deep, dark secret, then you don't tell it, right?"

"Okay, I'll settle for a shallow, light secret. Got any of those?"

Lisa chewed her bottom lip. "Do you promise not to laugh or make fun?"

"Sure."

"I mean, really promise?"

Georgie gave Lisa a push, nearly knocking her off the bed. "What's with you?"

Lisa didn't answer, so Georgie held up her right hand. "All right. I promise not to laugh or make fun. Girl Scout's honor."

"Are you a Girl Scout?"

"No."

Both girls laughed.

Lisa reached under her bed and brought out a locked box. "I write a lot. I write poems, or just write in my journal, whatever I feel like."

"That's it? That's your big secret?"

"You promised not to make fun."

"I'm just asking. Okay. I'll start over. *Why* is that a secret?"

"I . . . dunno. I mean, I have to write stuff down or I would explode with all my thoughts. I know that. What I don't know is why I can write things but I can't say them. And after I write them, I don't want anyone else to read them."

"I'd rather have my fingernails pulled off than write about my feelings, but if you like doing it, that's cool. So, are you going to let me read one of your poems?"

Lisa sat back, looking stunned. "No! I mean, I told you I do it. That's the secret."

"You don't trust me."

"Georgie, don't. I don't even let Carla read them."

It really wasn't that big a deal. But Lisa seemed so defensive about it. Georgie felt herself wanting to persist until she won.

"I'm not Carla. If you trust me, you'll let me read one."

Lisa looked at the box. Georgie could see a vein throbbing in her neck. She stared until she felt Lisa giving in.

76

Lisa lifted the lamp on her nightstand, pulled a key from under it, and unlocked the box.

"Whoa!" Georgie said. "We're talking high security here!"

Lisa seemed to ignore her. She searched through the box, letting her long hair form a curtain between her face and Georgie's. She brought out one sheet and, with a shaky hand, gave it to Georgie. Georgie read:

GYM CLASS

I wish I could put wings on my sneakers
to soar through the air
and make the volleyball
become a blur.

I wish I had an invisible helmet
and metal wristbands
so tears wouldn't sting my eyes
when I hit the ball.

I wish I wore a bodysuit
that hid my lack of . . .
everything
that every other girl has too much of.

I wish everyone else could be blindfolded
so that, just once, I could shower
and not feel like the freak
that I am.

Lisa was poised on the bed, waiting for Georgie's reaction. Actually, Georgie was surprised. The poem was real. It was what Georgie felt but would never in a zillion years admit.

"This is outta sight!" she said.

"Really?"

"Yeah. It's cool. I could never write something like that."

Lisa's face glowed. "Which part did you like?"

Suddenly, Georgie didn't want to compliment Lisa's writing even if it *was* good. Georgie couldn't stand someone who acted like a panting dog, needing attention. So she stood up and said, "You got a clock in here?"

"It's 8:55," Lisa said.

"My mom said she'd be back at nine. I've gotta split."

"Oh." Lisa held her hand out for the poem.

Georgie stood, crunched the paper into a ball, and threw it at Lisa, hitting her in the chest. "Bull's-eye!"

Lisa's head was lowered and her hair had fallen around it, so Georgie couldn't see her face. But she could see Lisa gently pressing the paper flat with the palm of her hand. Something about the tender way she rubbed the paper made Georgie feel rotten. She knew that poem was important to Lisa. Why did she have to be so mean sometimes?

"Hey, Lisa. Do you think I could have a copy of that poem?"

Lisa didn't look up. "Why? You obviously didn't think much of it."

"Because I tossed it at you? That's just a habit I have. Haven't you noticed the papers in my locker? They're a mess!" She sat down beside Lisa. "It really is good and all. I could copy it at home and bring it back to you."

Lisa peered at Georgie through her hair. She looked so hurt. Normally it would make Georgie mad, but Lisa had been nice to her tonight. She shouldn't have treated something that was special to Lisa so carelessly.

"How about it?" Then she made herself say, "Please?"

Lisa looked at the paper, then back at Georgie. "Well . . . okay."

"Thanks!" Georgie folded it neatly and put it into the back pocket of her jeans. She'd keep the poem for a few days, tell Lisa she'd copied it, and give it back. She stood, thinking how much easier this would have been if she hadn't been a jerk to begin with.

Lisa followed her down the stairs, but Georgie stopped short in the living room. Lisa's mom was folding clothes on the couch. Georgie hadn't planned on being polite to a grownup.

"Hello! You must be Georgie. Lisa said you would be by tonight." Her mom jumped up. The folded clothes spilled from her lap as she stood, but she didn't seem to notice.

"Hello, Mrs. Loutzenhiser. Thanks for having me over," Georgie said in her nicest voice.

"Leaving so soon? I meant to bring you girls a snack." She fluttered her hands. "I'll get one right away."

"Thanks, but my mom will be here any minute."

"Oh! Then I'll hurry. She can join us." She rushed out of the room as if she had to put out a fire.

"Is she always like that?" Georgie asked Lisa.

"She wasn't," Lisa said. "But lately she's been pretty jumpy."

"Why?"

"She and Dad . . . they fight a lot these days." Lisa tucked her hair behind her ears. "Ever since Alan . . . left home. And Carla went to college."

Before Georgie could ask any more questions, Denny swooped into the room and grabbed a small bra from the clothes basket.

"Give me that, you little worm!" Lisa chased him. As he ran, he put the bra on top of his head and fastened the hook under his chin.

Lisa lunged. Denny sidestepped her and yanked the bra off, stretching it out like a slingshot. "Anybody got any marbles? Nah, they'd be too big. Anybody got any BBs?"

Georgie said, "I thought you said he was shy when you had friends over."

"Well, he *used* to be."

Denny jumped onto the coffee table, holding the bra just out of Lisa's reach as she leaped for it. "Hey, Lisa," he said. "I heard Ma call this a training bra. So what are you trainin' 'em to do, anyway?"

"Knock it off!" Lisa shouted.

"If I were you, I think I'd be training 'em to *grow*," he said.

Georgie laughed. Lisa's mom came in with a tray of food and drinks. Denny hopped off the table and threw the bra at Lisa. He grabbed a soda from the tray and ran out of the room.

"Ma, you have got to make him stop! He's a mental case!"

"He's ten, Lisa," her mother said.

"He's funny," Georgie said. Lisa shot her a look. "In a mental kind of way," she added.

Georgie looked out the window. "Mom's here. Thanks for having me over!" she yelled as she ran to the car before Mrs. Loutzenhiser could stop her.

Georgie reached the car and turned to wave at Lisa, who was standing on the porch. The moon was full tonight, throwing its glow on Lisa's upturned face as she waved goodbye. Georgie's thoughts flew to her dad. It made her feel worse about Lisa's poem. Maybe she really would copy it. And make sure Lisa saw the copy. That ought to make her happy—and wipe away the guilt Georgie felt.

10 Georgie stomped down the hall beside Mrs. Donovan on Tuesday afternoon. Didn't this woman have enough to do?

"May I ask you a question?" Georgie said.

"Certainly."

"Are you crazy?"

Mrs. Donovan laughed. "Well, I suppose that depends on whom you ask. But if you're asking if *I* think I'm crazy, then, no. Do you think I am?"

"Yes," Georgie said. "Definitely."

Mrs. Donovan held her door open. Georgie hesitated. She thought about simply walking away, but then she saw Mr. Gordon watching her from his office.

"Georgie!" he said. "I hear things went smoothly at the Sunset Home."

"Uh-huh," Georgie said. "They did."

He looked at her over the top of his glasses. "Glad to hear it. Keep up the good work."

"Sure thing." She turned into Mrs. Donovan's office. Getting called to the principal's office over that stunt wasn't so terrible, but she didn't want to get into real trouble with him.

Georgie grabbed the back of a chair and faced Mrs. Donovan. "Listen, Mrs. D., I don't want to come here. I won't talk to you anymore."

"Great minds think alike," Mrs. Donovan said. "I don't think it's beneficial for us to talk, either."

Georgie threw out her arms. "Then why am I here?"

"Oh, several reasons," Mrs. Donovan said. "I promised your mother I would have these meetings with you."

"She stopped asking if I've seen you. We could just skip it."

"We could. But I promised, and I always keep promises. Besides, she asks *me* if we've talked."

"You two seem to be real friendly," Georgie said. "How about you just talk to each other and leave me out of it?"

"Let me guess," Mrs. Donovan said. "You were going for funny again."

Georgie glared at her.

"Another reason I brought you here is that I need help. Having students do good deeds for Glendale was a wonderful idea, but keeping track of everyone's projects is quite a job, and I'm afraid it's fallen on me."

She moved to a table in the corner, where papers were stacked, and sat down. "I was about to pull my hair out when I remembered that you wanted to escape home ec." She winked at Georgie, but friendly was the last thing Georgie wanted to be.

"Anyway, I thought we'd help each other. I'll pull you out of home ec one day a week if you'll work for me. How does that sound?"

"What's the catch?" Georgie asked.

"You're very smart, aren't you, Georgie? Well, there *is* a

catch. I know how much you hate talking about your dad so I bought this for you." She picked up a thin, red book.

Georgie reached over and took it from her. The pages were blank.

"I want you to write one feeling about your dad's being gone, and then we can get busy on these forms."

"Hey, no problem," Georgie said.

She sat at Mrs. Donovan's desk. No way was she going to write down her feelings. They were hers and she wasn't sharing them with anyone.

She decided to draw a picture of Mrs. Donovan instead. Georgie angrily grabbed a pencil, but soon lost herself in the rhythm of strokes. She sat back to look at her work. It was a good likeness of Mrs. Donovan, with her glasses and curly hair. Her eyes were open but unseeing. Georgie had drawn a noose around Mrs. Donovan's neck, her head at an angle. Georgie was past the point of caring if she got into real trouble. She was ready to get Mrs. Donovan off her back for good. If this picture didn't scare her away, nothing would.

She put the open book in front of Mrs. Donovan with a flourish. "There you go!"

Mrs. Donovan closed the book without looking and pushed it toward Georgie. "Oh, it's not for me," she said. "I don't want to see what you've written."

"But you have to!" Georgie said.

Mrs. Donovan looked up at her. "No, I don't. It's for you, Georgie. Is what you wrote how you really feel?"

"Oh, yeah." Georgie thought of the picture of dead Mrs. Donovan. "It's how I really feel."

"Great!" Mrs. Donovan smiled at her. "Let's get busy. We receive completed forms once a week from the places where the students do their good deeds. The forms tell us if the students showed up and how many hours they worked that week. Unfortunately, not everyone sends in a form, so I need to know whom to call. I'll check off the businesses or individuals who sent theirs in and pass the forms to you. Your job is to mark each student who worked at least two hours last week."

Georgie looked at the list and saw her own name. "Don't you realize I could put down that I worked whether I did or not? I could put down that *everyone* worked two hours! I could probably advertise and kids would pay me to do that."

Mrs. Donovan picked up a stack of papers. "Yes, I suppose you could."

Georgie started at the top and checked each name without bothering to see if the student worked at all. She checked all names beginning with *A* through *D*, keeping one eye on Mrs. Donovan. She expected Mrs. Donovan to stop her or yell or something. But Mrs. Donovan didn't say anything. She didn't even look to see if Georgie was doing what she was supposed to do.

Georgie started to mark the *E*'s, but it was too boring. Finally she erased the fake check marks, grabbed the first pile of forms, and checked off the students who really had done their job.

"Mrs. D.?"

"Yes, Georgie."

"You sure know how to take the fun out of things."

Georgie was walking in the crowded hall at the end of the day when she heard Lisa's voice.

"Georgie!"

She saw Lisa making her way through the rowdy kids, who were clearly anxious to escape for the day.

"We were assigned kitchens in home ec," Lisa said when she caught up with Georgie. "Because you weren't there, they stuck me with someone else!"

"Bummer," Georgie said.

"Where were you?"

"At the guidance counselor's office." Georgie threw her books into the locker and kicked it closed with her foot.

"Why?"

"Guidance, I suppose."

"Seriously," Lisa said, "why were you there?"

"It's where they send the messed-up kids." Georgie walked toward the exit.

Lisa squeezed her books to her chest. "But, Georgie, you're not messed up! You're the most together person I know."

"Yeah, that's me, all right." Georgie sneered and slid a sideways glance at Lisa. She was thrown when she saw the open expression on Lisa's face. Lisa really thought she was "together." It had been a long time since anyone had treated Georgie as if she weren't a problem.

"Well, what she really wanted was help with the Good Deeds project," Georgie said. It wasn't a complete lie.

"Oh! That sounds like fun. Does she need anyone else to help?"

"No, I think it's only a job for one." Georgie thought about that stupid book Mrs. Donovan wanted her to write her *feelings* in. "But it's just one day a week during home ec. So maybe it's a good thing you have another cooking partner, since I won't be there all the time."

They reached the line of buses. Georgie's hadn't pulled up yet, so she waited with Lisa.

"I should just get on the bus with you. We could call my mom from your house. She could pick me up after the brats go home."

"No!" Lisa looked panicky. "That's not a good idea."

"Sorr-ee!" Georgie said. And Lisa had just made her feel good about herself. "I didn't realize having me over last night was such a bad thing!"

"It's not that. I told you, my parents fight a lot."

"Which I don't get at all. I mean, Alan moved out of the house. What's the big deal?"

"It's not just that he moved out . . ." Lisa faltered.

"What's the rest of the story?" Georgie said. "Where *is* Alan?"

"There, uh, isn't any more to it."

Georgie could tell that Lisa was lying. "Lisa, where is Alan?" she persisted.

Lisa looked down.

"Look, tell me or I'll get on your bus, ride to your house, and ask your mom myself."

Lisa raised her head, her eyes open wide. "No! Alan is in—Chicago."

"So?" Georgie said.

Lisa lowered her head so that her hair covered her face. "He's in Chicago. And—Dad's afraid he's using LSD and smoking pot and stuff. So please don't talk to my parents about it, okay?"

"Okay. Geez, you could have said that all along."

Lisa quickly climbed onto the bus. "See ya!"

Georgie's bus still hadn't arrived. She watched Lisa find a seat beside a window. Georgie waved goodbye, but even from the sidewalk she could see that Lisa's face was pale, and she didn't look back at Georgie.

11 Three Saturdays later, when Georgie and Lisa walked into the Sunset Home, Camille was sitting behind the front desk, reading a newspaper.

"Anything good in there?" Lisa asked.

"Nothing good, girl. Nothing good," Camille said. "But then, what did we expect when we put that Richard Nixon in office?"

Lisa reached past her for the sign-in paper and pulled a pencil out of the drawer. Georgie sat on the corner of the desk as Lisa filled in her name and time on the sheet. She handed it to Georgie to sign. Georgie glanced at the record of their visits. After the first week, they'd lasted more like four hours than the two hours that were required.

"Do you guys realize we've been coming here a month?" Georgie said.

"Feels like you're part of the furniture, doesn't it?" Camille said.

Lisa laughed. "It does seem like we belong here."

"Like we're ancient and decrepit?" Georgie hopped off the desk and bumped a stack of flyers. "Oops!" She picked up the papers.

"Here, take one," said Camille. "We're having an open house in two weeks. These are to get the word out. Lord knows, these folks need visitors."

Lisa read one of the flyers and said, "Georgie, the open house is the last day of our project."

"So? We'll visit then anyway."

"I know, but a lot of people will be here. It would be nice if we got Sophia a corsage and dolled her up."

Georgie put the stack back on the desk. "You know I don't like doing that kind of stuff."

"I'll take care of everything. It'll be fun."

Georgie blew a strand of hair out of her face. "Well, since it *is* the last day we'll be here, I guess it's okay."

A sad look came over Lisa's face. Georgie had a feeling Lisa would come forever, but Georgie was ready to do as she pleased on Saturday mornings again.

"Hiya, Pearl," Georgie said as she walked past an elderly lady sitting on the sofa.

"Hi, Pearl," Lisa said. "How's the poncho coming?"

"Hello, girls." Pearl put down her knitting needles and said, "Why, Lisa, you would not believe how much easier a poncho is to make than a sweater. I'm so glad you told me they're the newest thing. My little great-granddaughter is going to be so surprised."

Georgie tapped her foot, then folded her arms. Lisa could talk to these coots all day if no one stopped her. "I'm going to find Aggy," she said. Georgie had gotten to know them all, but Aggy was still the only one she really liked.

Georgie walked into the rec room.

"Hi, Georgie!" Aggy called when she saw her.

"Hi, Ag." Georgie flopped down beside her on a couch. "What's goin' on?"

Aggy looked sad. Another resident, Emmaline, sat next to her in her wheelchair, nodding off.

"Nothing," Aggy said. "They won't let us turn the television on yet."

Man, Georgie thought, *you have to follow other people's rules when you're a kid and when you get old, too. What a raw deal.* Georgie watched one of the men, Arnold, slowly refold the paper he had been reading and drop it into a box full of newspapers. That gave her an idea.

"Aw, who needs television!" Georgie forced her voice to be light, knowing that no one needed a television more than she did. "Wouldn't you rather have a snowball fight?"

Aggy clapped her hands. "Oh, yes!"

"Aggy," Georgie said, "you wad up those newspapers. Arnold, give me a hand with this sofa."

By the time Lisa pushed Sophia's wheelchair into the rec room, two elderly men and three women were in position on one side, holding sofa cushions and big pillows as shields. On the other side, Aggy, Georgie, and even Camille were hidden behind the sofa frame.

Both sides had piles of wadded newspaper balls that they were throwing at one another. Besides Sophia, the only other person at the Sunset Home in a wheelchair was Emmaline. Georgie had talked her into being the referee. She sat at one end of the room with a baseball cap on her head and a whistle in her mouth. Emmaline looked official and kept blowing her whistle even though Georgie wasn't sure she understood the rules.

"What on earth?" Sophia said.

"Sophia!" Aggy jumped up and immediately got hit with a paper ball. "We're having a snowball fight!"

"This is so cool!" Lisa said. "Georgie, was this your idea?"

Before she could answer, Georgie heard Sophia sniff. "Maybe Georgie, maybe Aggy," she said. "They're like two peas in a pod, you know."

Georgie rose to answer Lisa and got smacked by a stream of snowballs. "Hey! They've got a ringer on their team!"

Arnold, on the other team, yelled back, "Betty played first base in the church softball league for thirty-five years!"

Georgie gave a phony look of surprise and cried out, "You're gonna get it, sister!" She and Aggy stood up and threw with both hands. One of Aggy's wild pitches hit Sophia on the side of the face.

Things quieted considerably. Sophia sternly said, "Lisa, please give me that wad of paper and wheel me closer."

Georgie watched as Lisa gave Sophia the paper ball and wheeled her beside Emmaline.

Sophia held out the ball and said, "Aggy? I believe this is yours."

Oh, great, Georgie thought. *Leave it to Sophia to be a wet blanket.*

Aggy bowed her head and came out from behind the couch. She walked slowly toward Sophia like a child who knew she had done something wrong.

Georgie let her go but swore to herself that if Sophia chewed Aggy out, she was going to step in. When Aggy was a few feet from the chair, Sophia cried, "Get her!" and beaned Aggy on the head with the wad. Everyone on the other team pelted Aggy.

Camille crouched down, holding her sides with laughter. Sophia barked, "Get me to the other side!" Lisa quickly pushed Sophia, almost toppling her as she ran to the safety of the sofa cushions.

"No fair! They've called in new recruits!" Georgie cried out, laughing as Lisa and Sophia grabbed their share of paper balls and joined the fight.

Afterward, Lisa told Georgie she'd wheel Sophia back to her room, because she tired easily. Georgie and Aggy cleaned up the mess. When they finished, Camille turned on the television. Aggy practically hopped onto the couch, she was so excited. If there'd been any news on, Georgie would have stayed. Since it was much too early in the day for that, she set out to find Lisa.

Lisa was with Sophia out on the patio.

"Oh, Georgie. I'm glad you've joined us. Isn't it lovely weather?" Sophia tilted her face toward the sun and closed her eyes.

Georgie took a deep breath. The sun felt warm and the

scent of flowers was still thick. It was a welcome smell after the stale air in the home. "Yeah," she said, "it's hard to believe it's October."

"I do dread winter," Sophia said. "I'll miss coming out here."

Georgie felt a little friendlier toward Sophia. "Um, Soph, it was cool the way you joined in the snowball fight."

Sophia chortled. "I knew I'd surprise you most of all, Georgie."

"Yeah, I didn't know you had it in you."

"Human nature is a pretty complex thing," Sophia said. "Not everyone is the same all the time."

"I guess," Georgie said, feeling a speech coming on. She should have kept quiet.

"Where is Aggy?" Sophia asked.

"Probably napping," Lisa said.

"Are you kidding?" Georgie said. "She's watching television. I doubt she ever naps."

"Aggy has always had more energy than any three people. Certainly more than I," Sophia said.

"She is . . . different . . . from you, isn't she?" Lisa said.

"Oh, dear, that's certainly an understatement."

"Hey, don't bad-mouth Aggy," Georgie said, "just because you don't like her."

"Don't like her?" Sophia said. "I adore her! I have for years and years."

"Really?" Georgie said. "I mean, like you said, you're just so different."

"You said 'years and years,' " Lisa said. "Does that mean you knew Aggy before coming here to live?"

Sophia said, "Dear, I've known Aggy since we were both young brides."

Lisa sat on the lawn bench. "How did you meet?"

"Oh, it wouldn't interest you."

"No, really, I'd like to hear the story."

By now Georgie was a little curious, too. "Go ahead, Soph. We've got nowhere else to be."

"Well, if you insist," Sophia said. "My husband and I bought our first house a long time ago. We were young and thrilled to be in our own home. Then our new neighbor introduced herself—Aggy Jensen. At first I was happy to have a friendly neighbor my age. But, oh, my! She nearly drove me crazy, that Aggy. She was as generous as the day is long, but she couldn't take a hint if you broadsided her with it.

"I'd always been a private person and wanted to stay that way, but Aggy would drag me to Tupperware parties or insist that she had to have my opinion on something so I'd feel forced to shop with her. She simply wouldn't leave me alone."

Georgie moved closer to Sophia. Lisa pulled her legs up and rested her chin on her knees.

"She did some crazy things in those days. Some people thought she was touched in the head."

Lisa said, "It doesn't sound like she's changed much."

"Well, she really is a little strange now. She's getting older and had a mild stroke last year. But I knew there was nothing wrong with Aggy before. She was just a free spirit. Then, after my husband died, I had my accident and was put in this thing." She pointed to her wheelchair. "I needed help. I had no family here, so I put our little house on the market and made plans to move to the Sunset Home. By then, Aggy lived alone, too. As soon as I told her my plans, she immediately called my real estate agent and told him he had to sell her house, too, because she would not let me live here 'alone.' "

Sophia's voice cracked and tears pooled in her eyes. "That was the single most selfless thing anyone has ever done for me."

"That's a neat story," Lisa said.

"Yeah, it is, Soph," Georgie said.

Sophia cleared her throat and sat up as straight as ever. "Yes, well, there is a point to it, you know. The point is, life would be easier without people like Aggy, but it would be so dull."

Georgie saw Lisa look at her with a funny expression. "What?" she said.

Lisa jumped a little, as if startled. "Nothing," she said. "I was just thinking that things aren't ever dull with you around, either."

Georgie snorted but knew that the sun wasn't the only thing making her feel warm.

Georgie was still feeling good when she got home that afternoon. She hadn't finished her weekend homework and needed to read a chapter of science and one of social studies. She took the books outside, knowing the cool days of winter would soon be here, and sat on the grass to read.

A shadow fell over her book. Georgie shaded her eyes and looked up at Mom.

"Hey, what say we go out for supper for a change?" She handed Georgie an open bottle of Coke.

"Great!" Georgie said. She took a sip and asked, "Where are we going?"

Mom sat on the ground next to her. "I'll let you pick the place and I'll pick the time."

"Time?" Georgie was wary. She ran her finger around the rim of the bottle. "Why a special time? Why not right now?"

"Well, we can leave now." Mom began twirling Georgie's hair, something Georgie had grown to hate. She set her bottle down and swatted Mom's hand away.

"Let me guess," Georgie said. "We can leave now, but we won't get back until the news is over, right?"

Mom sighed and began plucking grass. "Georgie, let's not get into all that right now. We don't have the babies tonight and we never go out. Let's just leave it at that and enjoy ourselves."

"Okay, but we either wait for the news to be over or get home before then, okay?"

"No news, sugar."

Georgie slammed her science book shut. "Then forget it."

"Georgie, you're going to drive yourself insane if you don't stop looking for your daddy on the TV. I've made up my mind to stop you one way or another. It's for your own good."

"My own good?" Georgie yelled. "You don't know anything about what's good for me!"

Georgie grabbed her books and jumped up, sending a spray of soda across the grass.

Monday had been a long day for Georgie. It seemed that every teacher thought he or she was the only one Georgie had. She hadn't had time to catch her breath all day, so she dragged her feet on the way home from school. She hoped the brats were still napping because she wasn't in the mood to deal with them. She turned the handle to open the kitchen door and caught a ball right in the chest. Before she had time to react, John jumped up, yelling, "Fall down! I got you!"

"You little monster!" Georgie yelled.

"But I got you," he said with less conviction.

"You are dead meat." Georgie tossed her books aside.

"No, *you* dead." John began backing away from her. He turned to run. Georgie caught him and pulled him into the living room.

"Mom!" she screamed. "Keep this troll away from me!"

When her mother didn't answer, Georgie called louder, "Mom!" She looked around the room. Somehow it felt bigger. Then she saw why. The television was missing.

Mom came out of the bathroom with a kid slung on her hip. She didn't give Georgie her usual cheery greeting.

"Where is the TV?" Georgie asked.

Mom walked over to a crib and put the baby inside.

"Come here, John." Mom crouched. He ran into her arms. She stood up, while John buried his face in her shoulder. "I sold it," she said.

"*Why?*"

"Because it's not healthy the way you watch it."

"The way I watch the news, you mean. The way I look for Dad there."

"Georgie, you know how I feel about this and you still won't quit."

"Because I love him!" Georgie cried. "It looks like I'm the only one who cares about him at all."

Georgie ran to her room and locked the door. Mom knocked on it, calling her name. Georgie ignored her. She grabbed her small duffel bag and threw some clothes inside. She couldn't stay here with Mom tonight, and there was only one place Georgie knew to go—Lisa's. She started to open her door and remembered Lisa's poem. She stuck it in her back pocket and walked out of the room.

"Where do you think you're going?" Mom said.

"I'm sleeping at Lisa's house tonight."

"You are not leaving here mad and you are not sleeping anywhere else on a school night, Georgie!"

She walked over to her mother. Because Georgie was taller, Mom had to look up, which was good for Georgie's strategy.

"I don't want to be here and you can't make me stay."

"I'll call Lisa's mother and tell her to send you straight back home!"

"No!" Georgie yelled. "You talked about me to Mrs. Donovan and now you want to tell Lisa's mom about me. It makes me feel like a freak! I'll have Lisa call so you'll know it's okay. She won't lie to you."

Mom said, "Georgie, can't you see? Things will just get worse if you leave now. *Please* stay and let's talk about this."

As Georgie shoved her books into the bag, she wanted to shout "I hate you!" But she didn't because Dad wouldn't have wanted her to. That was the only thing that kept her voice even. "You act like my feelings matter so much, but you don't really care what I think at all. You got rid of the TV to hurt me."

She grabbed the bag and stormed out of the house. As she stomped down the sidewalk, she heard the door open. John called out, "Georgie! Come back! I sorry I got you, Georgie!"

She slowed for just a second, then hurried away.

It was a long walk to Lisa's house. *I should have taken the bus,* Georgie thought. *If only I hadn't been so mad.* She switched her bag from one hand to the other as it got heavier. She took a shortcut through Willow Park, stopping to guzzle water from the drinking fountain, then climbed on top of a picnic table to rest.

Georgie stayed there, fuming over her mother's act, until hunger gnawed at her. She looked at her watch and was surprised to see how late it was. It would be after five by the time she reached Lisa's. She picked up her bag again and turned her thoughts to what she would say to Lisa and her family. It would be fine if Lisa, her mom, or even Denny answered the door. She didn't have a clue about what she would say to Lisa's dad. As long as he didn't answer, she would be all right.

She set her duffel bag on the porch and rang the bell. Lisa's dad opened the door, holding an unfolded newspaper in one hand. This was definitely not Georgie's day.

"Yes?" he said.

"Hi, Mr. Loutzenhiser. I'm Georgie Collins, Lisa's friend. Is she in?"

"She went to the store with her mother." His eyes squinted. "Who did you say you were?"

"Georgie Collins. Lisa and I just became friends this year. But good friends," she threw in for good measure.

"I see."

Georgie shifted from one foot to the other. When it didn't look as if he was going to let her in, she said, "You remind me a little of my dad. He has the same haircut."

Mr. Loutzenhiser held on to the doorknob and said nothing.

Georgie tried again. "Were you in the Air Force? Lisa mentioned you used to serve. My dad is a major. He's in Vietnam right now."

Mr. Loutzenhiser's face softened. "Well, now." He cleared his throat. "Well, well. Won't you come inside? I was an Army man, myself. But the Air Force is a fine branch of the military."

Relieved, Georgie decided to push her luck and tell a small fib. "Lisa invited me to spend the night so we could study together. We're partners in a project at school. I brought my duffel bag."

"Bring it in, bring it in," he said. He refolded the newspaper while Georgie brought her bag inside.

"I'll show you to Lisa's room."

"Thank you, but I know where it is," Georgie said. "I'll wait on the porch if that's okay with you."

"Certainly! Absolutely." He rubbed his hands together. "Well, it's wonderful that Lisa's made such a good new friend."

"Thank you, sir." Georgie gave him her best smile.

By the time Lisa came home, Georgie was relaxed enough to give a convincing performance.

She greeted Lisa's mother first. "Hi, Mrs. Loutzenhiser! Thanks a bunch for letting Lisa and me study together. Lisa insisted I bring my stuff for overnight, so I did, but I wanted to make sure it's all right with you first."

Georgie saw Lisa out of the corner of her eye. She

could have sworn Lisa's mouth was wide open, but Georgie concentrated on Lisa's mom.

"Oh! Of course! We'd love to have you, Georgie. I hope you like roasted chicken. If not, I think there's some leftover meat loaf. Or maybe I can whip up a small batch of goulash." Mrs. Loutzenhiser talked to herself as she walked into the kitchen.

"Chicken will be fine!" Georgie called after her.

"I call dibs on the drumsticks," Denny said as he followed his mom into the house.

Lisa didn't say a word. Georgie thought she might be in shock.

Georgie pounded her on the back. "Breathe!"

"It's not that I don't want you here, but why *are* you here?" Lisa said.

"Aw, my mom and I got into a fight. Hey, that reminds me. I need you to call her and tell her it's okay if I stay."

When Lisa didn't say anything, Georgie looked hard at her. "You don't really want me here."

"It's not that. It's just that things are so . . . tense around here."

"Still?" Georgie remembered Lisa saying that before, but it was weeks ago. "Why?"

"I—" Lisa started to say something, then seemed to change her mind. "Who knows."

"Well, I know why they're tense at my house and I'm not going back there tonight. Come on! It'll be fun,"

Georgie said. "Now, go call my mom before she calls the cops."

Lisa dragged her feet but followed Georgie inside and dialed her number.

"I'm coming!" Denny yelled as he rounded the dining room corner and slid into his chair between his dad and Lisa.

"Let's see them," his dad said, reaching for Denny's hands and turning them over.

"What? I washed!" Denny said.

"Yes, I see. Next time you might dry them, too." He looked at Denny, then tilted his head toward Lisa.

Denny squirmed in his chair. Mr. Loutzenhiser cleared his throat purposefully and Denny said, "Okay, okay." He grabbed Lisa's hand as if it were a live snake.

Lisa linked hands with her mom. Mrs. Loutzenhiser reached for Georgie's hand. Georgie looked at Lisa, confused, but Lisa just smiled at her, as if this were normal. So Georgie gave her hand to Lisa's mom, who gave it a squeeze. Mr. Loutzenhiser reached for Georgie's other hand. Now the family formed a circle around the big dining room table.

Lisa's dad began his prayer. "Lord, we thank you for this food, for our health, and for our brave soldiers fighting to keep us safe. Amen."

Georgie kept her eyes open during the prayer. She saw Lisa look sharply at her, then duck her head. Mrs.

Loutzenhiser looked pale and her lips were pressed together tight.

Mr. Loutzenhiser said, "Honey, you never mentioned that your new friend's father was an Air Force man."

Lisa's face contorted into a painful-looking smile. "I didn't? I thought I did."

"Georgie tells me he's fighting in Vietnam."

"Gene, please," Lisa's mom said. "Let's not discuss the war at dinner."

"I just think it's nice to see a little patriotism, that's all, Marian." He stabbed his piece of chicken.

Mrs. Loutzenhiser changed the subject. "Georgie, would you like broccoli?"

"Thanks." Georgie took the bowl. Geez, Lisa wasn't kidding when she said things were tense here.

Lisa's mom continued. "We usually have more dishes to choose from when we have company. We're happy to have you, but I wish Lisa had given us a little more warning."

Lisa's face turned bright red. "Sorry, Ma."

"I'm afraid we only have one biscuit each."

"That's fine, Mrs. Loutzenhiser. Really, this is just great." Georgie wished Lisa's mom would relax.

Denny put a biscuit on his plate, leaving the last one. He started to pass the plate to Lisa, hesitated, then coughed right onto Lisa's biscuit. "Sorry about that," he said with a sly grin. "Man, my germs are all over it now. Guess you won't want it."

Lisa's face fell.

"Really, Denny!" Mrs. Loutzenhiser said. "Next time please cover your mouth."

"Sure, Ma." He plopped the biscuit onto his plate. Georgie heard him whisper to Lisa, "Too bad for you, stickpin."

"You're so mean," Lisa said.

"And you're ugly," Denny said. "I can always act nice, but nothing's gonna make you cute."

Georgie waited for Lisa to say something back, but instead she bit into her piece of chicken. Denny buttered his biscuit, turned to Georgie, and chuckled. She glanced at his parents. Their heads were bent over their plates as if they were so wrapped up in their own thoughts they didn't even notice their kids.

After dinner, Mr. Loutzenhiser said, "You'll have to visit more often, Georgie. It's good to see some loyalty to the good old U.S. of A. in this house. Good, indeed." He squeezed Georgie's shoulder and walked into the television room.

Georgie wanted so much to follow and beg to watch the news. But Lisa's dad thought she was here to do homework. She had the feeling he was pretty strict about that stuff, so she figured she'd better forget about the news tonight. Maybe she could come back now that there wasn't a TV at home. He'd said she should visit more.

Georgie followed Lisa to her bedroom and sat at the window. She had as good a view of the moon from here as if she were outside.

Lisa still hadn't warmed to Georgie's unexpected visit, so Georgie decided it was time to pull out her big gun. She unfolded Lisa's poem, got out her notebook from her duffel bag, and began writing.

"Hey, that's my poem!" Lisa said.

"Sure, it is. I told you I wanted a copy. Sorry it's taken me so long." Georgie looked at Lisa with what she hoped was a sincere expression.

"Oh! No problem! I forgot you'd taken it."

"And I forgot I had it."

Both girls laughed.

"There." Georgie laid down the pen and handed Lisa the original poem. "Thanks."

"You're welcome!" Lisa looked happy as she put it back in the box with the other poems.

Georgie closed the notebook with the poem inside and put it in her bag. It was a small price to pay to get to spend the night away from Mom.

Georgie walked over to Carla's bed. "Think your sister will mind me using her bed?"

"No, she hasn't been home in almost a month."

Georgie looked at the wall. The newspaper articles about Kent State stared back at her. She knew she should let it go since she had bullied her way into sleeping here tonight, but she just couldn't.

"Look, I appreciate the bed and all, but I can't stand this." She yanked the tacks out and laid the articles face-down on Carla's dresser.

"That's okay. I probably won't put 'em back. If Dad saw them, he'd blow up anyway."

Georgie climbed into bed. Fighting with her mom had taken more out of her than she'd realized. Later, she didn't even remember saying good night to Lisa.

Georgie cracked open one eye, not sure if she had heard something. She turned onto her stomach. Then she heard Lisa cry out. Lifting up onto her elbows, she saw Lisa throw back her blankets and spring at Denny.

Awake now, Georgie saw Denny's eyes widen as he sidestepped her. He dropped a string and turned to run. Lisa fell to her knees, groping for whatever he had dropped.

Georgie leaped from her bed and pounced on Denny, dragging him to the floor.

"Are you nuts?" he said. "Get off!"

"Not until I hear what's going on," Georgie said.

Lisa pushed her hair off her face and panted. "Talk!"

"What? I didn't do anything," Denny struggled. Georgie pulled him up and let go.

"Liar!" Lisa said.

Denny lunged toward the door, but Georgie grabbed him.

"I just went to take a whiz and thought I heard some- one call my name," Denny said. "The next thing I know, Lisa's yelling and you're all over me."

"Ooh!" Lisa growled, obviously too mad to get the words out of her mouth.

"What really happened?" Georgie asked her.

Lisa breathed deeply and said, "He tied a string to my journal key and swung it to tickle my face! If I hadn't woken up, he would've had my key!"

Georgie rubbed her eyes, still gritty from sleep. "Is that all? Denny, beat it."

Denny scrambled out the door.

Lisa said, "You let him *go*? This isn't any of your business, Georgie!"

Georgie crawled back into bed, resting against the headboard. She pulled the covers over her knees and said, "Go back to sleep. It's only five-thirty, for heaven's sake."

"I'm too mad."

"Listen. I know that journal is some big deal to you, so Denny has to know it, too. If he knew the key was under your lamp, he could come in and get it any old time, right?"

"Yeah. So what?"

"So that means Denny wanted you to know he was taking it."

Lisa finally threw herself back onto her bed. "Okay, then why did he do it?"

"To get your goat. Geez, Lisa. You have *got* to stop letting people get to you. If you don't stand up for yourself, you'll be pegged for weak your whole life." Georgie plumped the pillow. "Grow a backbone, will ya?"

Lisa sat there, letting it sink in. Then her eyes grew big.

She jumped off the bed and onto all fours, feeling around. When she found the key, she ripped the string off.

"I'll try, but first I've got to find a better hiding place."

She rubbed her hand over her headboard. She finally found a small crack in the wood, just big enough to slip the key into.

Georgie grumbled from beneath her covers, "Would you go back to sleep!"

"Okay, but only so I can dream about wrapping my fingers around his scrawny neck until the last breath leaves his body."

"Just don't talk in your sleep," Georgie mumbled.

"How about I drop you girls off at school?" Mr. Loutzenhiser said at breakfast. "That duffel bag will be hard to handle on the bus."

"Thanks, Daddy," Lisa said. "It's a long ride."

Lisa and Georgie got into his backseat. Georgie had thought about calling her mom before they left but didn't know what to say. When she realized Mr. Loutzenhiser was taking a route that was a few blocks from her house, she asked him if he'd stop by so she could drop off the bag.

When she got out of the car, Mom was outside, helping John out of his mother's car.

John saw her first. "There's Georgie!"

"Oh, Georgie!" Mom said. She threw her arms around Georgie and this time Georgie hesitated only a second, then hugged her, too.

"Lisa's dad is taking us to school and I've gotta hurry."

"Okay, let me have this." Mom took the bag from Georgie and walked over to the car. "Thank you for taking good care of my daughter."

"No problem," Mr. Loutzenhiser said. "It was a pleasure to have her."

"So, I'll see you after school, okay?" Georgie said.

Mom smiled and nodded.

Georgie pushed her cap back and knelt beside John. It had eaten at her that he thought she left because of him. "And you, big guy, are getting very good at being a soldier."

"I am?" John asked.

"Yep, you got me good yesterday, didn't you?"

He nodded. "But you left."

"Not because you hit me with a ball." Georgie stood. "I have to get to school now, so you'll be in charge of the house until I get back. Think you can handle that?"

"Yeah!"

Georgie saluted him. He saluted back with a face that was beaming.

Stopping at Georgie's home had made the girls tardy. Since they had already missed most of homeroom, they hung out at Lisa's locker until it was time for first period.

Georgie said, "Hey, Loutzenhiser, I just wanted to say thanks. I mean, I know I put you on the spot last night but I had fun. And I could have, you know, done worse picking out a new friend."

Lisa grinned and threw her arms around Georgie. "Oh, me, too!"

"Yeah, well, you don't have to get weird about it." Georgie shrugged her off, even though she didn't really mind.

When homeroom ended, they walked to social studies class. Mr. Hennessy wasn't there yet. Maybe they'd have a substitute! Subs usually gave study time instead of a lesson. Georgie brightened at the thought, so she ran a few steps ahead of Lisa and slid to her desk as if it were home base.

She hadn't really done it for laughs, but the quiet in the room was sobering. Was Mr. Hennessy in the back? She looked around. No teacher. Kathy Newman's desk was empty, and Angel, who always sat behind her, was softly crying. The boy next to Angel looked pale.

Georgie glanced at the other kids. "What's going on?" she asked. Lisa sat at her desk. She shrugged. No one answered. Georgie could tell most of them were without a clue.

When the bell rang, Mr. Hennessy shuffled in.

"Hi, guys," he said quietly. He usually bounced into a room so animated you wondered if his clock was wound too tight. Something was definitely up.

112

Mr. Hennessy scooted papers back from the edge of his desk and sat on the corner.

"Some of you've heard, but for those of you who don't know . . ." He took a deep breath and started over. "Look, guys, there's just no easy way to tell you."

Georgie felt dread pulling her deep into her seat. Maybe he'd just announce that there was a pop quiz or that they were all flunking or something.

"Kathy Newman's family got word last night," he said. "Her brother, Brian, was killed in Vietnam."

Someone gasped. Angel began sobbing. A girl ran over and hugged her.

Georgie didn't know Kathy's brother, but, God, she didn't want to hear he'd died. Especially not in Vietnam. She looked at Kathy's empty desk. Then she looked at Lisa. Her hands covered her face, and she was clearly crying.

"Man, I remember Brian. He held the school record for the mile run," the boy in front of Georgie said. "He was a cool guy."

"Yes, he was," Mr. Hennessy said. "I taught him."

He went to the board and began writing. "Get out a sheet of paper, please, and write down Kathy's address. You or your parents might want to send a note of condolence."

At that moment Georgie wanted her dad more than ever. She ripped a paper out of her three-ring binder, but instead of writing Kathy's address she wrote, "Dear Dad," hoping she'd feel a connection.

"Forget today's lesson," Mr. Hennessy said. "I think it's important that we talk about this."

Georgie wanted to shout, *Talk about the Congo. Or draw some stupid map of Sweden. Talk about anything but this.* She looked at her letter. Her hand hovered over the paper, as frozen as her brain. She wrote, "Dear Dad, please be alive." Then she began drawing a picture of a crescent moon.

"The thing that gets me," Craig said, "is that a groovy guy like Brian gets sent halfway around the world just to die protecting Vietnamese who are too lazy to fight for themselves."

"*Lazy* isn't the best word." Mr. Hennessy rubbed the bridge of his nose. "Untrained, maybe. Poorly equipped. Frightened."

Georgie began another drawing, of a full moon. She hunched her shoulders over her paper and pulled her cap low. She wanted the bell to ring so she could get out of there.

Craig said, "The Tet Offensive showed us it's a war we can't win."

"The Tet Offensive!" Mr. Hennessy came to life. He jumped off his desk and wrote on the chalkboard, *Tet Nguyen Dan.*

"Who can tell me what this is?"

"It's some kind of Vietnamese holiday, right?" Angel said, then sniffed.

"Not just a holiday. It's Vietnam's most important holiday! A day they would let their guard down, right? Only in

1968, the Vietcong launched a series of major battles on Tet that no one was prepared for. And here we Americans were, in front of our televisions watching this horrible fight."

Mr. Hennessy began pacing in front of the chalkboard. "The reality is that it wasn't really a military victory for the Communists. *But*—" He stopped and looked at the class. "But it *appeared* that way on television. It made the war seem impossible to win."

"Who cares if we can win it or not? We're losing guys like Brian every day in Vietnam." Craig leaned forward. "I'll tell you who I think the real heroes are. Those kids who died at Kent State for protesting the war."

Georgie pushed her cap back. She heard a pounding sound in her ears.

"I think our guys in Vietnam should just lay down their arms and walk out," Craig said.

"You make me sick, Craig." Georgie threw down her pencil. "You think it's that simple? We're already in this war. It's not something we can just undo. It's like saying, 'Whoops, Mom! Life's not a party, so I've decided I don't want to be born.' "

"It's not the same thing!" he shouted.

"Yeah, it is!" she yelled. "You think we can just walk out? What about the South Vietnamese people? Could you leave and let the Vietcong kill them? And what about when the Communists make their way here?"

"Don't tell me you buy what the establishment

says about having to stop them there before they come here."

"Yeah, bozo, I buy it." Georgie stood up. She towered over Craig. "My dad volunteered to fight there. He did it so Communists won't ever be on American soil. He did it to save your sorry ass."

Craig stood up, too. The stupid peace sign he always wore around his neck swung as he looked Georgie straight in the eye and said, "I'll send him a thank-you note before we get word that he's been killed, too."

Georgie grabbed the peace sign and yanked. The leather string held for a second and then snapped. Craig lost his balance when it broke. She tossed the necklace and wrapped her hands around his throat. Georgie heard people yelling. Some tried to pull her off. Craig's eyes bulged and he clawed at her hands. She hung on until Mr. Hennessy finally pulled her away.

"That's enough," he said. "This has gone too far."

He shoved Georgie into the nearest desk and pushed through Craig's friends. "Someone get a wet paper towel!" he called out. "Are you okay, son?"

"Yeah." Craig rubbed his neck. A girl ran in with dripping paper towels, but Craig pushed them away. He looked embarrassed by the attention.

Mr. Hennessy turned to Georgie. "What about you? Are you all right?"

Georgie rolled her head from shoulder to shoulder. No pain.

"Sure," she said. She thought of her survival strategy. *Second standing order completed.*

She reached for her cap on the floor and dusted it off.

"Everyone sit down," Mr. Hennessy said. "Show's over."

The sounds of feet scuffing and desks opening brought a sense of normalcy to the room. Mr. Hennessy walked up to Georgie and caught her by the shoulders. "You could have really hurt Craig," he said.

Georgie shrugged.

"You realize you can be expelled for starting a fight." Mr. Hennessy stared at Georgie.

She looked away, knowing he was right.

"And you, Craig, as wrong as Georgie was, you provoked that attack. I want you to apologize."

Craig's face was white. He kept his eyes on his desk. "I shouldn't have said that about your dad but I disagree with you both." He looked at Georgie. "Maybe you're right. Maybe it's not a simple thing to undo. But you won't see me there if I'm drafted. I'd defect to Canada before I'd fight."

"You'd lose your citizenship," the boy next to Georgie said. "You couldn't come back and live here later. That's heavy, man. You'd better be sure you know what you're giving up."

"I've already thought about it. I don't want to live in a country that's involved in a war as wrong as this one. I'll burn my draft card just like Alan Loutzenhiser and escape to Canada."

Alan Loutzenhiser?

Georgie turned her puzzled eyes to Lisa's pale face. Lisa grabbed her books and ran from the room as the bell rang.

Georgie felt herself filling up with that bad feeling again as she thought of all the time she'd spent with Lisa. She's lied and said Alan was in Chicago. Georgie thought she would burst with anger and betrayal.

She threw open the door to the girls' restroom, where she had seen Lisa go. Lisa was standing inside, but after one look at Georgie she went straight into a stall. Georgie's chest heaved. She needed to calm down because right now she was mad enough to tear the stall door off its hinges.

Georgie splashed cold water on her face and wiped it on her sleeve. She tried to make her voice sound normal. "So your brother defected."

Lisa slowly came out of the stall. "Yeah, I guess that's what they call it." She raised her eyes to look at Georgie. She seemed scared.

Good, thought Georgie. *She* should *be scared.*

The blood pounded in Georgie's ears. "And you didn't see any reason to tell me that, huh?"

"Well, sure. I mean, I thought about it. I guess I was afraid you would hate me. I really like us being friends and I didn't want anything to ruin that."

"Really? Friends?" Georgie leaned back against a sink and crossed her arms. "They sure do have a funny definition of friendship in this school. I never thought *friends* told each other lies! You said he was in *Chicago*!"

"Well, gee, Georgie."

" 'Well, gee, Georgie,' " Georgie said mockingly.

"Look at how you're acting now that you know," Lisa said. "This is what I was afraid would happen." She walked to another sink, away from Georgie, to wash her hands.

Georgie looked Lisa up and down, from her tie-dyed blue-and-yellow shirt to her blue miniskirt. Her boots hugged her calves and came up to her knees—the same kind of boots that everyone was wearing. Her clothes, so painstakingly put together and so . . . boring. Now everything, *everything* about Lisa made her sick.

"Tsk, tsk. Perfect little Lisa, with her color-coordinated world, telling lies."

"Georgie, please stop."

" 'Georgie, please stop.' "

"That's *enough*!" Lisa said.

"What are you going to do about it? Tell your Communist-loving brother? Oh, wait! How could I forget? He can't help you because he *ran away to another country!*"

"Georgie, please, I never meant for this to happen. I shouldn't have lied and I should have told you about Alan. But I've never intentionally hurt you. At least I never tried to get you into trouble like you did to me."

"When did I get you into trouble?"

"You know, with Mr. Gordon."

"You call that trouble? Geez, you are such a baby, Lisa. That was nothing. If you want to see trouble, you'd better watch your back."

Lisa quickly turned away. She fumbled with the paper towel she had used to dry her hands, covered her right hand with it, and reached for the door handle. That was the last straw for Georgie. Lisa was such a loser she couldn't even make a grand exit. Georgie reached past her, grabbed the handle with her bare hand, and blasted out of the restroom.

With the strong disinfectants the janitors used, Lisa was stupid to worry about germs. At least Georgie *thought* they used strong ones. What else could be causing her eyes to well with tears?

That night Georgie sat on the porch as the moonlight poured over her like a soft blanket. It was the first time she'd let her guard down today. She'd been so mad at Lisa that she'd felt like a small tornado ripping through the school. With that attitude, no one had talked to her and that's exactly how she wanted it. The one time she saw Lisa, she thought Lisa would keel over from fright. It almost made Georgie laugh to think about it.

"Sugar?" Mom said through the door. "Lisa's on the phone."

"Tell her I don't want to talk to her."

"Georgie!" Mom said. "What happened?"

"Nothing *happened*. She's just not who I thought she was," Georgie said. "She's not my friend."

"Georgia, I am not going to be rude to her and neither are you. If you've got a bone to pick with Lisa, come do it yourself."

Georgie stretched out in a relaxed position and tried to ignore her mother, but she knew Mom would outwait her. Mom could be a big old bully. Georgie finally got up and stomped inside. She grabbed the receiver and slammed it down on the cradle.

"Georgia Francine!"

"That's my name, don't—" Georgie was about to say, "Don't wear it out." But she knew she was treading on thin ice with Mom, so she finished with, "Don't tell me if she calls again. I really won't talk to her."

The next morning, Georgie found a letter that had been shoved into the vent on her locker. She pulled it out and saw "To Georgie" in Lisa's swirly handwriting. She'd drawn a little heart over the i. The heart was such a cutesy Lisa thing, it almost made Georgie gag. She didn't want to read an apology or an explanation. Georgie ripped the letter into minuscule pieces without opening it. She waited until Lisa was away from her locker and shoved all the pieces into the vent. Lisa would have a nice surprise when she opened it later.

At lunch, Georgie slid her food tray next to Angel. "Mind if I sit here?"

"Yes, I do mind," Angel said. "I will not eat with Lisa Loutzenhiser."

"Cool!" Georgie said. "Neither will I."

Angel reared back and looked at Georgie. "I thought you two were best friends."

"I'm new here. I didn't know about her brother."

Angel sniffed and picked up her sandwich. Georgie didn't really like Angel. She acted so stuck-up, as if her sweaty gym socks smelled like rose petals. Still, she was Kathy's best friend. Georgie felt herself thinking about Kathy a lot lately. She told herself it was because they both hated Lisa, not because they'd both had someone in the war.

Georgie asked, "So how is Kathy doing?"

"As well as can be expected." Angel let out a huge sigh and put her sandwich down as if she couldn't eat another bite, when she'd been wolfing it seconds before.

Geez. Georgie wondered if befriending Kathy was worth the effort. "Well, when is she coming back to school?"

"She'll probably be here tomorrow. She needs the support of her friends right now. Besides, it will take one or two weeks for Brian's body to be flown home for the funeral." Angel wiped at her eyes, but Georgie didn't see any tears.

"I'm glad to hear she's coming back," Georgie said. "Well, gotta go!" She hopped up, anxious to get away from Angel.

Kathy returned on Thursday. Angel and a herd of girls surrounded her everywhere she went. President Nixon didn't have that much security. Georgie finally wrote her a note.

Hi, Kathy,

I'm really sorry about your brother. I didn't know that Lisa's brother was a spineless draft dodger until the other day. She's not my friend anymore. Maybe we could talk sometime? My dad is in Vietnam.

Georgie

She passed the note to Kathy in social studies while Mr. Hennessy had his back turned. Kathy read it and gave Georgie a slight smile.

Saturday morning came, and Georgie made it to the Sunset Home an hour before the usual time. She was sitting across from Sophia in the recreation room, studying the white backgammon pieces, when she heard Lisa's voice in the hall.

"Hi, Emmaline."

"Hi, buttercup."

"Do you know where Sophia is?"

"Last I saw of her, she was headed for the rec room."

"Thanks," Lisa said.

Georgie moved her pieces, capturing Sophia's black one.

Camille said in her drawl, "Mmm, mmm, it does look like you've met your match, Sophia."

"Yes, it does." Sophia chuckled.

Camille looked up. "Well, looky here. Lisa came, after all."

Georgie stared at the pieces.

Lisa said, "Of course I came. I always come."

"Georgie didn't think you'd make it today," said Camille.

Georgie sat up straight and looked at Lisa. She wanted to get Lisa's reaction to her shirt. It was her dad's green military shirt with the name "COLLINS" sewn onto it.

Lisa glanced at it and looked away.

Sophia turned from Lisa to Georgie and seemed to sense the tension. Well, how could she not? It was as thick as fog.

"Lisa, come sit beside me," Sophia said.

Lisa slid close to Sophia and held her hand. Georgie wanted to puke. Sophia and Lisa were both such prissy bores.

"I didn't know you liked backgammon, Sophia," Lisa said.

"Oh, I love it! And what a treat to have Georgie offer to play with me. I must confess, I was beginning to think she only came to see Aggy." Sophia winked.

"Aggy's neat. But I want to visit you, too." Georgie gave her fake smile.

"So, what have you two girls been up to this week?" Sophia asked.

Georgie waited to see what Lisa would say. When she didn't answer, Georgie said, "I got a letter from my dad. I thought you might like to hear it."

"I would love to, Georgie! What a nice thing to share it with us, isn't it, Lisa?"

Lisa nodded but looked sick.

Georgie took a piece of paper from her pocket and unfolded it. " 'Dear Captain,' " she began.

"Wait, who's this captain?" Sophia asked.

"It's me," Georgie said. "Ever since I was little, my dad has always given me a rank, just one below his. When he was captain, I was first lieutenant; now that he's a major, I'm captain. He says that means I'm in charge when he's away."

"How delightful!" Sophia said. "Please read on."

Georgie read aloud:

"Dear Captain,

"Mom told me you're not too excited about this move. I wish you'd told me when I was there. Guess you were being a good soldier and not complaining. I don't blame you, kiddo. I'm not too excited about the places they keep moving me, either. Just remember my promise. The last time we re-upped was the last time. Soon I'll be home and you'll be so tired of me and bored with living in the same spot, you'll be ready to ship me back over here.

"Don't forget your promise, Captain. You keep things

running smoothly on that end, and I'll do my job here. Soon we'll be together. I'll send my love to you tonight. Don't forget to look for it.

Dad"

"Oh, dear." Sophia sniffed into her handkerchief. "That was lovely, Georgie. Wasn't it, Lisa?"

Lisa plucked at the frayed hem of her bell bottoms and murmured, "Yes, it was."

"What did he mean by sending you his love tonight?" Sophia said.

"It's just a little thing. Something between the two of us." Georgie hoped her tone let them know she wouldn't answer any more questions. Some things were meant to be private.

"Well, it's a double blessing because a letter means he's safe as well as letting you hear from him," Sophia said.

"Yeah," Georgie said. "You can almost forget that he's in a jungle, going on missions, getting shot at every day. You can almost forget he's there to protect us, can't you, Lisa?"

It was the first time Georgie had said something directly to her in days.

Lisa took a deep breath and said, "He sounds like a nice man."

Georgie's eyes flickered, but just for an instant. Then she snorted.

"I . . . never mind," Lisa said.

"What, dear?" Sophia asked.

"I must have misunderstood. I thought Georgie said she just got that letter."

"She did. Right, Georgie?"

"Yeah," Georgie said. "So?"

"So you moved here in May. I wonder why he would write about something that happened months ago, that's all," Lisa said.

"Have you ever seen Vietnam? Have you ever bothered to even watch it on the news? Do you think there's a mailbox on every corner?" Georgie shouted.

"I've watched the news." Lisa's face was all splotchy. "I know it's awful for your dad. I don't know why you're so mad at me."

Georgie jumped up, but Sophia pushed her wheelchair between them. "Girls, please! You don't want to fight over this. Goodness, there's already enough fighting over the war. Are you two having problems of some sort?"

"No, Soph. Of course not. Lisa and I are close. We're just like this." Georgie wrapped two fingers together.

15   Mrs. Donovan didn't have to track her down anymore. Georgie gladly went to her office on Tuesday afternoons to get out of home ec.

"Hello, Georgie," Mrs. Donovan called from the table in the corner.

"Hi, Mrs. D." Georgie sat at the desk and opened her red book. She wrote, "Jingle bells, shotgun shells, Halloween is here. Easter Bunny came last night and brought a case of root beer."

She smiled as she closed the book. She wrote something bizarre every week, since Mrs. Donovan never looked at it.

"You're smiling. You must have written good thoughts of your dad."

"Yeah," Georgie answered. "Really good thoughts of Dad."

"That's great." She turned to the worktable. "Well, I must say, we're finally getting cooperation from the community. I think everyone on the list mailed in their forms this week."

"Groovy," Georgie said, and began checking off students' names. When she came to Lisa's, she said, "Mrs. D., we don't have to do our project together, do we? Just as long as we do it?"

"Are you asking if you have to do it with your partner?"

"Yeah." Georgie ran the pencil inside the bandana she'd tied around her hair and scratched her head with it.

"Are you and Lisa having problems?" Mrs. Donovan asked.

"That's not an answer to my question. I just want to know if I can go to the Sunset *asylum* by myself, as long as I put in my two hours."

128

"Well, no, Georgie," Mrs. Donovan said. "The whole point is that you work together with a student you didn't know before."

"Even if she's a liar? And conniving?" Georgie asked. "Even then?"

Mrs. Donovan sat back in her chair. "I don't know Lisa well, but I've heard excellent reports from her teachers."

"She's good at hiding things. They wouldn't know."

"You need to remember that part of this experiment is to determine if the project brings you closer to your partner," Mrs. Donovan said. "Your report should be honest. If you and Lisa don't get along, or if the project has hurt your relationship, you can write about that."

"So I can write that she's a low-down, lying traitor and it won't affect my grade?"

"Not if that's what you think she is." Mrs. Donovan looked as if she didn't really believe Lisa could be such a thing, but she didn't argue. She went back to her forms.

Georgie didn't feel like working. She doodled on the bottom of the form, making squares and filling them in with black lead. She wished she could tell Mrs. Donovan about Lisa keeping her brother a secret. She wanted to tell her how much she hated Lisa now, how much she wanted to hurt Lisa, to lessen the pain she felt. Georgie wished she hadn't closed the door between herself and Mrs. Donovan. But she knew that if she opened it, Mrs. Donovan would want Georgie to talk about her dad and she just couldn't.

Georgie colored so hard with the pencil that the lead broke. She got up to sharpen it and noticed the empty spot on the shelf. Mrs. Donovan had turned off the spotlight and, for some reason, that made Georgie feel worse instead of better. Mrs. Donovan probably loved her dad as much as Georgie loved hers.

She sharpened the pencil and sat back down. "Mrs. D.?"

"Yes, Georgie?"

"About your dad's ship . . . I . . . Do you have another one that he made?"

"No." She looked up, but her eyes weren't sad.

"I probably shouldn't have broken it," Georgie admitted.

Mrs. Donovan put down her pen. "Well, I had my dad for a while and he's gone. I had that ship for a while and it's gone. Things change. But I'll always love him and that won't change." She patted Georgie's hand and turned her attention back to the forms.

Georgie tried to get busy, too, but it was hard because everything looked blurry.

16 Georgie wasn't too thrilled about being part of Kathy's entourage, but it seemed impossible to get Kathy alone. Angel grated on Georgie's nerves something fierce.

As they walked down the hall, Angel would call out, "Let Kathy through!" and at lunch, "Let Kathy be first in line!" Georgie didn't know how Kathy stood it. Surely she was so shook up over her brother that she didn't notice how annoying Angel was.

At lunch, Kathy turned to Georgie and said, "Why don't you sit beside me?"

"Thanks!" Finally, she'd get to talk to her. Angel looked so jealous, it was almost worth the wait.

Georgie sat down. "I'm really sorry about your brother."

Kathy's eyes teared up and Georgie quickly added, "But we don't have to talk about it! I just wanted you to know."

"Thanks," Kathy said as she picked at her food. "I knew your dad was in Nam. I always wondered why you hung out with Lisa."

"She never told me about Alan," Georgie said.

"Hah! I'm not surprised." Kathy let her fork clatter against the tray. "Brian and Alan were friends. So were our parents. We were like one big, happy family. But living so close to Grissom, Brian was always anxious to enlist in the

Air Force. Alan tried to talk him out of it. They got into a fight over it."

"So your brother enlisted and Lisa's went to college," Georgie said.

"Right. The funny part is, Brian made straight A's in high school. He could have breezed through college, but not Alan," Kathy said. "When Brian got his orders to ship out, Alan had just flunked out of college and run off to Canada so he wouldn't get drafted." Kathy's voice shook. "He didn't have the guts to tell his family in person. He wrote that he wasn't going to be killed in a war, like Brian probably would. After that, Lisa thought things should just stay the same between us. But I hated Alan, and I hated Lisa for thinking that I could ever be around her again."

"That's how I feel," Georgie said.

"Look at her over there," Kathy said. "She's been with Craig Evans all day."

Lisa and Craig sat two tables over, their heads bent close together as they talked.

Georgie said, "Lisa told me you like him, too."

"Like him? I hate him. He's another coward. I only flirted with him to make her mad," Kathy said.

Georgie lowered her sandwich to her plate. Suddenly she remembered Lisa's poem. "I know how to make her really mad. Meet me outside in five minutes and I'll show you."

She picked up her tray, and Angel quickly scooted to

her spot. "Uh, make sure you meet me outside *alone*," Georgie said.

She ran to her locker. She kept it pretty messy. She'd always been in such a rush to walk Lisa to her locker that she hadn't kept hers clean, so it took a few minutes to find the notebook containing the poem. But there it was, on the very bottom. She pulled the poem from the notebook and ran to the picnic area outside.

She grinned when she found Kathy by herself. "You know how weird Lisa is about people reading her stuff," Georgie said.

"No," Kathy said.

"Back when you and Lisa were friends," Georgie said, "she told you about her poetry, right?"

Kathy seemed confused. "I don't know what you're talking about."

Georgie looked at the poem and an uneasy feeling settled in. It was so important to Lisa, yet she'd never told Kathy, who was her best friend. Lisa had barely known Georgie when she told *her*.

Georgie shook her head to clear it. "Look, it doesn't matter. What matters is she wrote this poem and doesn't want *anyone* else to read it."

Kathy's eyes lit up.

"Here." Georgie thrust it into Kathy's hands. "Read it. That'll drive her crazy."

"Thank you!"

"Yeah, well, I've gotta split." Georgie had just found a way to get back at Lisa. Why didn't she feel good about it?

Georgie went straight to Kathy's locker the next morning so they could hang out together before the bell rang, but Kathy wasn't there. On her way to class, she found Kathy at Angel's locker, deep in conversation. Then, as Thursday wore on, Georgie noticed that Angel went out of her way to stand by Kathy's side, always between her and Georgie.

Georgie thought she'd never get to talk to Kathy, but lunchtime came and Angel couldn't sit on *both* sides of her. "Boy, you're hard to get close to!" Georgie said as she slid next to Kathy.

"Angel is just taking care of me," Kathy said.

"I guess I forget how hard this is, with your brother's death and all."

"Oh, yes. She helps with that, too." Kathy frowned. "But I meant she's helping me plan a surprise."

"Oh!" Georgie said. "What kind of surprise?"

"If I told you, it wouldn't be one, would it?" Kathy said in a teasing tone.

Georgie bit into her sandwich. She felt bad about Kathy's brother and she knew that having a dad in Vietnam should make them close. But as lunch passed, she felt that was really the only thing they had in common.

The bell sounded, ending lunch period, and Georgie walked with Kathy and Angel to their lockers. Kathy opened hers and, for the first time, Georgie was close enough to see inside. Taped to the door was some teen magazine picture of Donny Osmond. That cinched it for Georgie.

"I'll catch up with you guys later," she said. *The next time it snows in August,* she thought.

Georgie kept to herself on Friday. She didn't seek out Kathy and her crowd, and she was relieved when they didn't look for her, either. Georgie's dad had been right: it wasn't a good idea to make friends with a group. Georgie just wouldn't have a friend at this school. It was no big deal. She felt a pang when she thought of Lisa, but shrugged it off.

She met Lisa and Craig in the hall, two yellow-bellied traitors spending time together because no one else wanted to be with them. She caught Lisa's eye and glared. Lisa turned pale and looked away.

Georgie walked into fifth period PE. The other girls always complained about their one-piece gym suit, which was about as ugly as prison garb, but Georgie couldn't care less what she wore. PE gave her a chance to burn off some of the hatred that seemed to fill her lately. She was really looking forward to working off some bad feelings today.

The construction at the school wasn't completely finished, so the girls' locker room didn't have lockers yet. Instead, there were sections with wire baskets, like the public swimming pool used, for gym clothes.

Georgie yanked out her basket, grabbing her ugly blue

suit and gym shoes. Lisa hung back until Georgie moved away, then hurried over to her basket and slid it out. Lisa picked up her gym suit and reached for her shoes at the bottom of the basket.

Then she let out a scream.

Georgie tried to ignore what was happening, but curiosity propelled her toward the girls gathered around Lisa's basket. In one of Lisa's sneakers was a dead bird, its wings spread wide. In the other shoe was a scrap of paper.

"What's wrong?" a girl at the back of the crowd asked.

Lisa didn't answer. She headed for the toilet but got only as far as the trash can. She retched, losing her lunch. Lisa wrapped her arms around her middle. Her teeth chattered and her whole body shook.

Someone yelled, "Get Coach, quick! Lisa's sick."

While everyone was paying attention to Lisa, Georgie reached for the paper in Lisa's sneaker.

GYM CLASS

I wish I could put wings on my sneakers
to soar through the air
and make the volleyball
become a blur.

"Wings on my sneakers," she whispered, and looked at the poor bird, one broken wing hanging over the side of the shoe. Georgie looked around. Kathy and Angel were the only two, besides her, who weren't hovering around Lisa. They were giggling and whispering to each other as they pulled on their blue suits.

The PE teacher ran in and wiped Lisa's mouth with paper towels, then wet a rag with cool water and put it on the back of Lisa's neck. "Come on, hon. Let's get you to the nurse." She gently led her toward the nurse's office. "The rest of you, get dressed and run laps until I get back!"

Georgie walked toward Kathy.

"Did you like that, Georgie?" Kathy asked. "Angel came up with the idea."

"To kill a bird?" Georgie said. She felt sick to her stomach.

"We didn't have to go that far," Angel said. "I live on a farm. The cats and dogs are always dragging up something dead."

The other students fled past Georgie and Kathy to the gym. Kathy turned to Angel and said, "Hurry!"

Before Georgie could react, Angel grabbed the poem from Georgie's hand, then threw some sheets of paper towel over the bird and scooped it into a sack. She quickly disappeared out the rear exit.

Kathy said, "She has to get rid of it before we get caught."

"So this is the big surprise you were working on." Georgie felt anger flaring up inside her. No wonder Lisa hadn't told Kathy she wrote poetry.

"What's the matter? You seem angry," Kathy said.

"I am!" Georgie said. "Look, I just gave you that poem to read. I mean, if you're mad at Alan, that's one thing. But Lisa didn't skip out on the war."

"I don't believe this!" Kathy put her hand on her hip. "You should thank us! She lied to you about Alan."

Georgie felt confused by her feelings, but one thing she was clear on: at least Lisa wasn't cruel. Right now Georgie was angrier with Kathy than she'd ever been with Lisa.

"Whatever Lisa did to me is between me and her. I don't need you or your sicko friend to help me." Georgie turned to leave.

Kathy's words caught her as she reached the door. "If you turn us in for doing this, I'll tell them you gave me the poem!"

"Kathy, I don't have to tell to get even," Georgie shot back. "Your best friend is Angel. That's enough revenge for me."

Because of her fight with Lisa, then Kathy, Georgie forgot about the open house at the Sunset Home until she saw the WELCOME banner stretched across the front porch. Balloons were tied to the pillars and, inside, the home looked festive.

Georgie pulled the sheet out of the drawer and signed in. Lisa's name wasn't on the list. Georgie wondered if she would come at all. Lisa must have gone home after getting sick in gym class yesterday—Georgie hadn't seen her since.

"You're a little early for the open house, aren't you?" Camille asked. "It doesn't start for another hour." She had changed from her uniform into a colorful floral dress and high heels.

"Lisa's plan. She wanted us to get Sophia gussied up before the guests came," Georgie said.

"That's awfully nice of you girls."

"Well, it's our last visit," Georgie said, wondering if that plan had changed.

The door to room 17 was open, so Georgie walked in. Sophia's chin rested on her hand as she looked out the window.

"Hey there, Soph," Georgie said.

Sophia jumped. "My goodness! I thought you would be here later."

"I'm sorry we didn't tell you we were coming early, but everything's okay." Before she could say another word, the door opened and Lisa walked in, carrying a small suitcase.

Georgie was surprised by how much relief she felt.

Lisa ignored Georgie and said, "Hi, Sophia!" She kissed her cheek. "Look what I brought." She opened the case and gently lifted out a pink orchid corsage surrounded with baby's breath.

"Oh, my!" Sophia said. "Such an extravagance!"

"You always look pretty in pink. You're going to be the

belle of the ball today. I brought nail polish, and, if you'll let me, I'll have your hair looking like a queen's."

Sophia seemed to relax. "Well, how could I pass up an opportunity to look like a queen?"

Lisa began brushing Sophia's hair, completely in control, as if nothing had happened yesterday. Georgie knew she should be relieved, but Lisa's attitude rubbed her the wrong way. She'd expected Lisa to be devastated, and Georgie had felt bad about hurting her. What a waste that had been.

"Girls," Sophia said, "you are the sweetest things to do this for me."

"It was all Lisa's idea," Georgie said, because taking credit for something she hadn't done felt like wearing a coat that was three sizes too small.

"But you're here, too, Georgie. Thank you," Sophia said. "Now, who's painting my nails? I feel like I'm at a luxury salon!"

"You don't want me to," Georgie said. "I've never painted a nail in my life."

Sophia dug the bottle of nail polish out of Lisa's case. "It's just like they taught you in kindergarten, Georgie. Try your best to stay inside the lines."

Georgie was almost finished when Aggy came in. She was wearing the same red dress and green hat that she had worn the first time Lisa and Georgie saw her.

"Guess what, Sophia? They have cake and punch," Aggy said. "Do you like cake, Georgie?"

"Yeah, Ag, but we're not staying." Georgie frowned as she tried to paint Sophia's thumbnail.

"I'll get you some now! How about a nice Hawaiian Punch?"

"Sure," Georgie mumbled.

Aggy pulled back and punched Georgie in the arm, sending a trail of nail polish up Sophia's arm.

"Hey!" Georgie yelled.

Aggy giggled and sang, "Fruit juicy Hawaiian Punch." Then she skipped out of the room.

Sophia's hand flew to her mouth, trying to cover her laughter. "Well, you did say 'sure,' dear," she said.

Georgie laughed. "She caught me off guard." Then she forced a bland expression because she didn't want Lisa to think she was in a good mood. She busied herself by wiping the polish off Sophia's arm.

Sophia held up her hands. "Georgie, you did a fabulous job! It's been forever since I've had a manicure. I might have to start getting one regularly."

Lisa held up a mirror.

"And, Lisa!" Sophia said, "I don't think my hair has ever been so fashionable."

Sophia tenderly patted her hair so she wouldn't smear her nails. Tears welled in her eyes when Lisa pinned the corsage to her dress.

"Girls, I can't tell you what a treat this has been for me."

Lisa kissed Sophia on the cheek and whispered, "You look regal."

Georgie felt uncomfortable with all the gushy thanks and kisses. She needed to get outside, so she said, "See ya, Soph."

"Enjoy your day," Lisa called out.

Sophia winked at them and waved goodbye.

Georgie walked quickly to the door and gulped in the cool October air. Lisa came out next and stood quietly beside her.

Lisa sighed. "I guess that was our last official visit here together."

"Right," Georgie said. "No reason for us to be together anymore. Just write your report, I'll write mine, and we're through with each other."

Lisa threw up her hands and said, "Fine!"

Georgie trudged toward her house. She was free of Lisa and free of the Sunset Home. She knew she should be happy, but her insides felt as empty as a deflated balloon.

She was almost at her house when she sensed someone following her. She turned and there was Lisa, the little suitcase banging against her leg as she hurried.

"Georgie!" Lisa set the case down and panted, trying to catch her breath. "Look, it's *not* okay that you don't want to write the report with me. We started this together and we're finishing it together, whether you want to or not."

"That sounds like an order!" Georgie said. If she hadn't heard it with her own ears, she wouldn't have believed it.

"Not only that, we need to get something straight," Lisa said. "I know you're mad at me. The whole world knows because you snub me every chance you get. Well, I can't help that what my brother did makes you mad."

Lisa put her hands on her hips. "Kathy's friendship wasn't all I lost when Alan sent that letter," she said. "Dad threw Alan's stuff away. Ma turned into some kind of robot, just working fast at stuff so she doesn't have to think about it. Carla became a peace activist, and Dad won't let her come home."

"You know what? I don't blame your dad," Georgie said.

"Then this should make you happy. He moved into the spare bedroom when we got word that Brian was killed. My parents talk about divorce a lot now. All because my mom said she'd rather have Alan alive in Canada than dead in Vietnam."

Georgie flinched. "Your brother broke the *law*! He let down a whole country."

"Right. *He* did that, Georgie. I didn't."

Suddenly Georgie's anger at Lisa turned to hurt. Weren't Lisa's words the same as the ones Georgie had used on Kathy just yesterday?

"But you should have told me. I told you right up front my dad was in Vietnam. You knew then that we couldn't have a friendship and you just kept your mouth shut."

Lisa nodded. "I know it now and I'm sorry. But I liked you and I— I don't know. I thought if you got to know me, maybe we could work through all that."

Georgie shook her head. They couldn't be friends anymore. Georgie started to leave.

"Wait! I was wrong, but I never tried to hurt you," Lisa said. "I trusted you with my poem. It's bad enough you used it to humiliate me, but you *killed a bird*!"

"Actually, nobody killed it, and I didn't put the dead bird in your shoe."

"Oh, for heaven's sake." Lisa threw her hands in the air. "You're the only person besides me who had a copy of that poem."

Lisa turned to go.

"Wait," Georgie said.

Lisa stopped. She kicked a rock with her shoe.

Georgie said, "You have to remember how mad I was. I mean, I could have strangled you, I was that mad."

"I know that," Lisa said.

"So . . ." Georgie took a deep breath. "I gave your poem to Kathy."

Lisa gasped and turned around.

"I know it was a lousy idea. But how could I know she'd use it against you? I mean, I was so mad at you! And you acted like your poem was *so* private. Like you'd just *die* if anyone read it. So I gave it to her. Kathy was the perfect person because, you know, she hates your guts."

"You don't get it, do you, Georgie? Kathy will probably always hate my family. That's not something I can do anything about. But you gave away my poem, knowing it would hurt. *You* did that to me."

"To read!" Georgie rose to her full height. "Not to haunt you with."

To Georgie's surprise, Lisa took a step closer. "She wouldn't have had the chance without you, though, would she?"

"I said I was sorry!" Georgie yelled. Then she turned and ran up the steps to her house.

"No, you didn't!" Lisa shouted. "We're not finished!"

Georgie threw her door open, and Lisa was right on her heels. Georgie stomped straight through the kitchen, then took two steps into the living room. She stopped so fast that Lisa bumped into her.

A man in an Air Force uniform with a major's bars on his sleeve was sitting on the couch with Georgie's mom.

Lisa saw him, too, and grinned like an idiot. "Georgie!" she said. "Your dad!"

18 Georgie couldn't move. Mom was sitting with him. She had to have known he was coming. Georgie felt so betrayed, she was sick.

He stood and said, "Hello, Captain."

Whatever had kept her from moving was instantly released. Georgie ran past Lisa, made it through the kitchen and over the porch steps in one jump, then dashed down the street.

She heard him calling her name. She ran faster. She went down side streets trying to lose him, but he kept up a steady pace. After a time she felt a pain in her side. She could hear the soft thud of his boots gaining on her. Up ahead she saw an alley between two lawns. She ran straight, as if to pass it, then ducked down the alley at the last minute, hoping to throw him off.

The gravel wasn't as easy to move on as the sidewalk. Still she ran, with the pebbles crunching beneath her shoes. She was just about at the end when her right foot slipped. She wobbled, slid sideways, and fell.

She was down only a few seconds, but it was enough. He grabbed her shoulders to help her up. When she tried to break free, his grip became as hard as steel.

"You can fight all you want, girl, but we're having a talk."

"No!" Georgie fought his hold.

He put one arm across her stomach and pulled her down with him. His hold was so tight it nearly knocked the breath out of her. Then he wrapped his other beefy arm across her shoulders and held her.

Georgie struggled to get away. Her legs were free, so she kicked at him until she didn't have any strength left. He still held her. She cried out of sheer frustration. She would have killed him if she'd had the chance.

Georgie sat panting. Finally her breath started coming at a normal pace. She became aware of the gravel biting into her bare legs.

"Listen, Captain."

"Don't! Don't you *ever* call me that!"

"I'm sorry, Georgie. I heard it so much, I got used to thinking of you as that."

"Stop!" Georgie said, then whispered, "Please don't say anything."

"Honey, I have to."

Georgie moaned. The major was still behind her with his arms around her. Holding her. Keeping her helpless.

God, how she hated him.

"Your mom told me you won't listen to her. She says she can't show you my letters or even say I've called. I know you don't want to believe it. I don't, either. Your daddy and I go way back, before you were born. He was my best friend."

Tears fell down Georgie's face. She couldn't fight anymore, but still he held on.

"I saw his plane go down."

"Shut up, Jack! Just stop it!"

She tried to jerk away, but he kept talking.

"I was his wingman, Georgie. My plane was flying right beside his and he didn't make it out of his plane. I'd have seen. It doesn't matter that they haven't found the crash site. I know in my heart he never could've survived it. I know it, Georgie. If I thought for one minute he'd made it, I'd comb every inch of Nam myself."

Now he was crying, too.

At first Georgie made a mewing sound, like a kitten, then sobs overtook her.

He finally loosened his grip and turned her around,

pulling her onto his lap the way he did when she was little. "It's okay," he said, rubbing her back. "Your daddy wouldn't mind your tears, Georgie. But he *would* mind that you won't let him go."

Georgie buried her face in the roughness of his jacket. From somewhere deep inside a cry made its way up. She could feel it trying to surface and couldn't stop it.

"No!" she wailed. "It's not true!"

He rocked her and smoothed her hair, cradling her as she cried. But in the end it didn't matter. He still said, "Yes, honey, it is."

Georgie sat on the steps, listening to Mom's and Jack's soft voices coming from the kitchen as she looked at the moon. She felt sad and tired. For months she'd been pushing against a door to keep it closed. Now that the door had been blasted wide open, she barely had the strength left to stand.

Mom came outside and said, "Jack is sleeping on the couch tonight, sugar. He said to tell you good night."

Georgie nodded, then asked a question that had been nagging her. "Mom? What happened to Lisa?"

"She called her mother to come get her." Mom opened the screen door. "Come sit with me for a minute."

Georgie sighed loudly.

"Oh, I'm not going to tell you to talk about your feelings," Mom said. "I have something for you."

Georgie stood and dusted off the seat of her skirt. She went into the kitchen and pulled out a chair across from Mom.

"Jack asked me to give you this," Mom said. "He sent me mine in July, after your dad's plane crashed, but he knew you weren't ready for yours. He would have given it to you himself, but he thought you'd had enough of him for one day."

Mom slid an envelope across to Georgie.

Dad's handwriting was on the front. Georgie picked it up, rose, and said, "Good night, Mom."

Georgie sat alone in her room, staring at the envelope. Dad made his letters stand straight up and down, almost like soldiers at attention. Georgie had gone through the mail each day for months, praying for a letter from Dad. Now that she had one, she didn't want to open it. She knew this was the last one she would ever get.

She threw on pajamas and brushed her teeth. She put the letter in a drawer, then crawled into bed.

She couldn't sleep. The letter called to her. Finally she opened the drawer, grabbed the envelope, and carried it to the window. She slid the paper out and rubbed her hand over it, knowing Dad was the last person to touch it. She carefully spread it open and read:

Georgie,

I hope you never see this letter. I'm writing it for Jack to give you in case I don't make it. If I know you (and I do), then I know you're mad at him for giving it to you. Don't be. He's following my orders and he'll be the one to look after you and Mom from now on.

As for you, Captain, we need to add a contingency plan, which is sort of a backup. Your contingency plan has three parts. One is to take good care of your mom. Love her enough for me, too. She hasn't had it easy living with two hardheads like us.

The second part is, don't make me into a hero. I know you love me, but I'm a stubborn soldier who should have retired so this wouldn't have happened. Think your own thoughts and follow your own mind, girl. You've got a good one.

The most important part is this. You've been my whole world since the day you came screaming into it. You're everything I see and everything I feel. Always remember that my love for you is bigger than life, Georgie. A little thing like dying isn't going to stop it.

With love always,
Dad

That night Georgie fell asleep on the floor, bathed in the moonlight, with her body curled protectively around Dad's letter.

* * *

Georgie stayed close to Mom the next morning. After months of feeling suffocated, being near her felt as comforting as a bandage on a raw wound.

After lunch, Mom said, "Since Jack is leaving this evening, he and I need to spend some time filling out papers and doing things that I've . . . put off. Tying up loose ends, I guess."

Georgie had a few ends to tie up herself.

First she went to the Sunset Home. She found Sophia on the patio, reading a book.

"Hello, Georgie!" She laid the book in her lap, then really looked at Georgie. "Is something wrong, dear?"

Georgie slumped on the bench beside her. "Soph, remember that letter I read you from my dad?"

"Of course!"

Georgie unbuttoned her jacket. "I lied when I said I'd just gotten it. He sent it last summer. It was the last letter he sent."

She handed Sophia Dad's letter. "Until this one."

After reading it, Sophia carefully folded it, put it back inside the envelope, and placed it on the bench beside Georgie. She patted Georgie's hand and waited.

Georgie said, "Mom told me his plane went down in July. But they couldn't find his body. I hoped he was still alive, trying to come back. I guess I pretended he was alive because I couldn't stand to think otherwise. Crazy, huh?"

Sophia sat back in her chair. "When my husband died,

151

I set the table for two at every meal and I talked to him just like he was sitting there."

She tucked her book into the side of her chair. "So, tell me, Georgie. Does that make *me* crazy?"

"Nah." Georgie's mouth lifted at one corner in a small smile.

"Time helps with the pain, dear," Sophia said. "But the hole in your heart may stay. Try to think of it as a good thing—a reminder of how much you love your father."

Georgie took a deep breath, releasing a little of the pain she'd been carrying as she exhaled. She carefully slipped the letter into her pocket.

She stood, unlocked Sophia's brake, and began pushing her inside. "So, what's it gonna be today? Backgammon or chess?"

"I'd love a game of backgammon."

"Okay, we'll play chess next Saturday."

"*Next* Saturday?" Sophia turned in her chair to look at Georgie. "Lisa said she was coming next week, but I thought yesterday was your last visit."

Georgie shrugged. "I don't know when it happened, but somewhere along the line I started really liking ya, Soph."

That evening, Jack kissed Mom goodbye on the cheek, then turned to Georgie. "Are you and I okay?" he asked.

"Yeah," Georgie said. "No sense in killing the messenger, right?" She grabbed Jack's bag; then she and Mom followed him to his rental car. "Besides, my orders say that you'll be taking care of us from now on."

Georgie slid her gaze to Mom. "Right, Mom?"

Mom nodded, with tears in her eyes. "I'm going to let you two say goodbye." She hurried toward the house. It hit Georgie full force how much Mom missed Dad.

Jack watched her go. "It's been hard on her, too, Georgie."

"Yeah," Georgie said. "I know that now."

"Will you read my letters from now on?"

"Yes," Georgie said. "I might even answer them."

"I'd like that." Jack put his bag in the trunk and turned to her. "Your mom wants to stay here, Georgie. She wants to open up that preschool. Is that good with you?"

"It's an okay place."

"You got friends here?" he asked.

"I don't think so." Georgie thought of Lisa. "There was this one girl, but we're just too different."

"Your daddy and I were your age when we met. We were like night and day. Fought like we hated each other. Then we became best friends." Jack slammed the trunk. "Now, I want you to let me know when you get yourself a best friend, okay?"

"Yeah, right."

"No, I mean it. You write and tell me in a letter. Deal?"

Georgie hesitated, then said, "Deal."

"I'll be looking forward to it."

After he left, Georgie thought about Jack's question. Did she have a friend? She found her mom at the kitchen sink.

"Mom, I have to talk to Lisa," she said. "Tonight."

This time Georgie waited until Mom completely stopped the car. She wasn't in a rush to hop out because she didn't know if Lisa would want to see her.

Georgie saw a figure making its way toward her and, even though it was dark outside, she knew it was Lisa.

She turned to Mom. "You're not going to *stay* while we talk, are you?"

Mom smiled. "How about I go for a drive?"

Georgie gave her a grateful hug.

"Hey," Georgie said to Lisa as her mom pulled away.

"Hi." Lisa folded her arms across her chest. "After you ran away yesterday, your mom told me about your dad. I'm really sorry."

"Me, too," Georgie said. She followed Lisa to the porch and sat next to her.

"You told me off pretty good yesterday," Georgie said. "When I told you to stand up for yourself, I didn't mean with me."

"You deserved it."

Georgie chuckled. Even if Lisa told her to get lost, she liked this tougher version.

"So why are you here?" Lisa asked, fingering a wisp of hair.

"I wanted you to know I saw Sophia today." Georgie cleared her throat. "I told her about my dad."

"You did?"

"Yeah, she was cool. I told her I'd still visit."

"That's great. I mean, I'm glad you want to go back."

Georgie pulled a chrysanthemum that was growing beside the porch and began plucking its petals. "Listen, the main reason I'm here is to say I'm sorry I gave Kathy your poem." Georgie sighed. "I guess there are a lot of things I'd like to undo."

Lisa took a deep breath. "And being my friend is one of them."

"Well . . . no. I can't stand Angel," Georgie said. "And Kathy got on my nerves. She *still* has a crush on Donny Osmond. Being around you is a whole lot better. Even when we're fighting."

Lisa smiled and hugged her knees to her chest.

"Your choice of crushes isn't much better than Kathy's, though," Georgie said. "I've noticed how you've been spending a lot of time with that peacenik Craig."

"You don't get it. I know some people call our soldiers killers. But Craig and Carla don't blame them. They just want the war to end before anyone else dies." Lisa's forehead furrowed. "I'm sure you don't want to hear this, but I do, too."

Georgie had felt all along that people were either for the soldiers or against them. Maybe Lisa was right and some just wanted the deaths to end. It was something for her to think about.

She gathered the fluffy petals, cupped her hands, and blew them toward the sky. They swirled in the moonlight, then floated to the ground.

Georgie's eyes smarted and she tried to swallow but couldn't. Tears spilled from her eyes.

Lisa put her hand on Georgie's shoulder.

"For a minute I almost forgot about my dad," Georgie said. "Vietnam is on the other side of the world. When it's night there, it's day here, so Dad always saw the moon before I did." She wiped her face on her sleeve. "He promised to send me his love on the moon, so every night I come out and look at it."

Georgie brushed the petals off the step. "I guess there's no reason to do that anymore."

Lisa chewed her bottom lip. "It was a way for you to stay close to your dad. Why should that change?"

Tears slid down Georgie's cheeks. "So, how long have you been this smart?"

Lisa grinned. "I've always been smart. You just weren't smart enough to notice."

Georgie smiled and gave Lisa's shoulder a shove.

Lisa shoved back.

Georgie saw Lisa leaning against Georgie's locker before she reached it on Monday morning. She felt her face break into a big grin. "Hey!" she said.

"Hi." Lisa looked sad.

"Is something wrong?"

"First tell me how you're doing."

"Better," Georgie said. "I've felt so angry that I wanted to hurt everyone around me. I don't feel that way anymore." She took a deep breath. "But I miss him so much."

Lisa was quiet for a minute. "In a way, we both lost our dads this weekend. Mine moved out."

"Why?" Georgie said.

"After you left last night, Carla called and said she wants to come home. Dad hung up on her and Ma got mad about it. Then they began arguing about Alan—again."

Lisa took a ragged breath. "I ran upstairs to escape their fighting. The next thing I knew, Ma came into my room to tell me that Dad was moving out."

She turned her bright eyes on Georgie. "It doesn't seem right. Your dad is gone, but he had no choice. My dad did."

Georgie closed her locker door, and they walked toward homeroom. Lisa was right: her dad had a choice. Nothing should keep a family apart but death.

"Where's your dad staying?" Georgie asked.

"In the back room of his store, Ma says."

"Store?" Georgie said. "I never knew he had a store. What kind?"

"A paint store. Premium Paints. You might not have seen it. It's here on the North Ridge side."

"Wait, I think I *have* seen it. It's on . . . um . . . I can't think of the street."

"Chestnut Street."

"Oh, yeah! Now I remember." Georgie thought she should become a detective.

The bell over the door chimed as Georgie walked into the paint store after school. One customer held fabric swatches next to paint chips. The way she frowned and stared at each one told Georgie she would be there a while.

Georgie walked toward a loud sound in the back. Lisa's dad stood next to a vibrating machine, which was shaking a can of paint.

He shut off the machine when he saw Georgie.

"Hello, Georgie," he said. "Lisa's not here. You'll probably find her at home."

"I know she's not here, Mr. Loutzenhiser. I want to talk to you about her."

He scratched beneath his chin. "Is she in some kind of trouble?"

"No, sir." Georgie laughed. "Lisa wouldn't know how to get into trouble."

He looked relieved and began stacking cans of paint on a shelf. "Georgie, let's get down to brass tacks. What's on your mind?"

He seemed so direct, but Georgie liked that. "Lisa is pretty upset that you moved out."

He looked surprised. "That's personal, young lady."

"Yeah, it would be except that she's my friend and I don't want to see her so sad." Georgie sat on a crate. "Mr. Loutzenhiser, I know you're mad at Alan."

"Georgie, I'm sure you mean well, but you're skating on some mighty thin ice," he said. "And you can tell my daughter to talk to me herself if she wants to know anything."

Georgie didn't budge. "I'm not sure she has anything to say to you, but I do. I want to tell you about my dad."

Still holding a can, Mr. Loutzenhiser stopped moving.

"His plane was shot and went down in flames last July. Witnesses didn't see him eject. They never found the plane wreck, so he's listed as missing in action. I didn't want to believe it for a long time, but now I know he's dead."

Mr. Loutzenhiser sat down heavily on a crate.

"The way I see it, sir, is that if I can accept Alan's choice, then I think you ought to do the same."

Georgie got up and hurried toward the door. It still hurt too much to talk about Dad, and she was afraid she would cry. When she reached the handle, she looked back. Mr. Loutzenhiser's face was buried in his hands.

Classes were suspended on Tuesday afternoon to give the Good Deeds for Glendale partners an opportunity to finish their reports at school and turn them in. Georgie was relieved, because it meant she wouldn't have to go to Mrs. Donovan's office. Georgie had figured out weeks ago that Mom had told Mrs. Donovan about Dad's death. Even though she knew Mrs. D. had tried to help her, Georgie wasn't ready to face her just yet.

The Good Deeds reports were to be graded and hung

in the halls by the end of the week. Georgie worried that she would be writing Lisa's and hers alone because Lisa had been absent that morning.

After lunch, she brightened when Lisa showed up in their homeroom and scooted her desk over beside Georgie's. "Boy, am I glad to see you! Were you sick?"

"Nope," Lisa said. "And I can't go with you to the Sunset Home on Saturday."

"But you're the one who wanted to go." Georgie scratched her head. "And why do you look so happy about it?"

"My dad came back last night!" Lisa said. "He came just to see Mom, but then they both talked to Denny and me. We stayed up late crying and talking things over, so Mom let us sleep in this morning."

"So he's home to stay?" Georgie said.

"We're going to see how things go, but, hopefully, yes. The great news is he said Carla can come home on weekends, so we're all going to pick her up on Saturday, which is why I can't go to the Sunset Home."

"Wow!" Georgie said. "I'm happy for you. But what about Alan?"

"Well, legally Alan can't come home." Lisa's smile faded a little. "But Dad is willing to talk to him if Alan tries to reach us again. So that's something."

"That's great, Lisa!" Georgie said.

"Yeah, it is great." Lisa's glow faded. "I'm sorry things didn't turn out well for you."

"Don't." Georgie held her hand up. "I'm truly happy for you."

"Thanks, Georgie."

"Who knows? Maybe if things get back to normal at your house, Denny will stop driving you crazy."

"Now, *that* would take a miracle!"

Georgie laughed.

Lisa reached for her notebook. "I just wonder what made my dad change his mind. He wouldn't say."

Georgie put her head down and began writing so Lisa couldn't see her face. "Geez, Lisa, I don't have a clue."

Two hours later, Georgie threw down her pen and sat back. "Finally! So much writing and all we really had to say was the project worked."

"Don't forget to include this." Lisa held out a paper.

Georgie took it and read:

WHAT I LEARNED FROM OUR PROJECT
by Lisa Loutzenhiser

One type of person
is like driftwood,
either torn from a tree
or wrenched from a ship,
just floating, adrift.

Another is like the sea,
with tides pushing and pulling,

waves pounding the shore,
seldom quiet,
rarely calm.

But when a piece of driftwood
gets caught up in the sea,
it will be tossed about,
worn and sanded,
battered and thrown.

After a bit, the driftwood changes,
it becomes polished, even beautiful.
The driftwood takes on new life
that wouldn't have been possible
if it weren't for the sea.

It was a good poem, but Georgie chewed her lip.

"What's wrong?" Lisa said.

"It's perfect, Lisa. But are you sure you want to?" Georgie asked. "They're hanging these in the hall for everyone to read. I'd hate for your feelings to get hurt."

Lisa said, "I need for Kathy and Angel to know I'm not afraid of what I write anymore."

Georgie smiled at Lisa. She looked at the clock, anxious to get home. She had promised John she would take him to the park. She still had ten minutes before school was dismissed. Just enough time to do one more thing. Pulling a sheet of notepaper from her binder, she wrote:

Dear Jack,

Remember that girl I told you about who was too different from me? I guess we kind of grew on each other. Anyway, I wanted you to know that I do have a best friend here.

Her name is Lisa.

20 Late Friday afternoon, Georgie waited at the line of poplar trees that ran between the faculty parking lot and school. Finally, she saw Mrs. Donovan come out, hiking her purse strap onto her shoulder. The trees were too young to hide Georgie, so she crouched beside a parked bus while Mrs. Donovan fumbled with the keys, slipped into her car, then pulled away from Glendale Middle School. Georgie picked up the sack at her feet and strode toward the office.

Mrs. Sanders had her head down, typing. Georgie watched as she plunked each key firmly on the old typewriter, then, with her right hand, pushed the carriage return to the left to begin the next line. Georgie cleared her throat. Mrs. Sanders looked up. When she saw Georgie, she gave the return a hard slap.

"Mrs. Donovan is gone for the day," she said, and went back to typing.

Georgie flashed a brilliant smile. "Mrs. Sanders, I feel we got off on the wrong foot."

Mrs. Sanders sat back and crossed her arms. "What is it you want?"

"For us to be friends?" Georgie said.

Mrs. Sanders snorted.

"Okay," Georgie said. "I need two minutes in Mrs. Donovan's office."

"You must be out of your mind," Mrs. Sanders said. "No."

"But—"

"No buts."

"Mrs. Sanders . . ."

"Georgie, I will report you if you do not leave immediately."

Georgie took a deep breath, then blurted out, "Mrs. Sanders, didn't you ever make a mistake?"

"Of course I've made mistakes," she said. "After all, I'm human."

"Well, I'm human, too," Georgie said.

Mrs. Sanders's face softened just enough to encourage Georgie.

"I have something to give Mrs. Donovan and I won't hurt anything and you can come with me and I won't be in there more than two minutes. I promise!" She caught her breath and added, "Please."

Mrs. Sanders scratched her nose and looked out the window. After what seemed like forever, she looked at Georgie. "If you touch anything . . ."

"I won't!" Georgie said.

Mrs. Sanders heaved herself out of her chair and pulled a ring of keys from a filing-cabinet drawer. She unlocked Mrs. Donovan's door and stepped inside.

Clutching her sack, Georgie followed.

Mrs. Sanders planted herself firmly in the middle of the room. She reminded Georgie of a sentry.

Georgie walked over to Mrs. Donovan's desk. Mrs. Donovan's satchel lay in the center of the desk. Remembering her promise not to touch anything, Georgie said, "Mrs. Sanders, would you please move the satchel?"

Mrs. Sanders reluctantly scooted it to the side.

Georgie gently lifted a small box from her bag. She flipped the lid up to reveal a bronze-colored cross hanging from a ribbon that was blue and white, with a red stripe down the center. She rubbed her finger over the cross, then reverently placed it in the center of the desk.

Mrs. Sanders rushed to her side, as if she thought Georgie might have planted a stink bomb.

Georgie reached back into the sack and pulled out the red book Mrs. Donovan had given her.

She had torn out the pages with the nonsense she'd been writing for the last five and a half weeks. All that was left was the page that Georgie had written that day. She read it one more time:

My dad died July 2, 1970. For a long time I didn't want to believe it but now I have to. In my heart it feels like

*he died this week. It hurts and I don't think it will ever stop
hurting.*

*This is one of his medals. It's called the Distinguished
Flying Cross Medal and is awarded for "Heroism or
extraordinary achievement while participating in aerial
flight." I'm sorry I broke your dad's ship. This medal means
as much to me as the ship meant to you. I hope you'll keep
it instead.*

She propped the open book next to the medal for Mrs.
Donovan to find when she came back to work on Monday.

She turned to go, but Mrs. Sanders said, "Not so fast."

Georgie's hopes plunged. In the last few days she had
thought a lot about how she could make it up to Mrs.
Donovan for destroying her father's ship and realized she
couldn't. Her remorse and the pain of losing her dad were
so raw that Georgie decided leaving the medal and book
would show Mrs. Donovan how she felt. Now it seemed
that Mrs. Sanders wasn't going to let her.

Mrs. Sanders reached past Georgie and picked up the
medal. "You've gotten fingerprints on it," she said as she
pulled her handkerchief from her sleeve and gently wiped
the medal. "There, now. It's nice and shiny."

Mrs. Sanders set the medal back on the desk. She put
her arm around Georgie's shoulder. "Much better, don't
you think?" She gave Georgie a rare smile.

"Yes, it is," Georgie said, and together they left the
room.

Georgie walked down the hall and had almost reached the front doors when Mrs. Donovan came bursting through. "Mrs. Donovan! I—I thought you were gone," Georgie said.

"It's been one of those days," Mrs. Donovan said. "One step forward, two back. I left my satchel on my desk."

Georgie swallowed hard. She thought she'd have the weekend to prepare for Mrs. Donovan's reaction. "Oh, well, gotta go!" Georgie called.

The crisp autumn air smacked Georgie in the face when she ran out the door. What kind of dumb luck was this? What if she'd taken just one minute longer in Mrs. Donovan's office? The thought sent a chill through her.

She rounded the corner and tried to quicken her steps. But Mrs. Donovan's office was right there; Georgie felt herself being pulled to the window.

Mrs. Donovan already held Georgie's red book in her hand. Despite the cool afternoon, Georgie's hands were sweaty. Mrs. Donovan's back was to her and Georgie couldn't see her face. Mrs. Donovan laid the book down and stood there, still as stone.

Georgie steeled herself. She would just have to take whatever happened next.

Mrs. Donovan picked up the medal. She held it a moment, then carried it to the bookcase. She set it on the shelf in the exact same place where the ship in the bottle had been. Then she turned on the small spotlight.

Mission accomplished, Georgie headed home.

Acknowledgments

Once again, I'm indebted to my agent, Steven Chudney, and to my editor, Beverly Reingold, for their hard work and faith in me. John J. Bonk, Lisa Williams Kline, Lee P. Sauer, Manya Tessler, and Laura Backes gave help and guidance throughout the writing of *Georgie's Moon*. Thank you, all.

I owe special thanks to Walter R. Griffin (2nd Battalion, 26th and 7th Marines, Vietnam, July 4, 1969–July 4, 1970) for sharing his firsthand knowledge of the Vietnam War.

Thank you to Wendell Minor, a man who surely paints with his heart, for the breathtaking jacket art.

It pains me, but I must reluctantly thank my mischievous brother, Mark Lincicum, on whom the character Denny is based. Mark majored in driving me crazy. He thinks I left out his best tricks, but truth is stranger than fiction—had I included them, no one would have believed me.